Caught
in the
Lie

Caught in a Lie

Sylvia McNicoll

Cover photo by
Rodrigo Moreno

Cover design by
Andrea Casault

SCHOLASTIC CANADA LTD.

Scholastic Canada Ltd.
175 Hillmount Rd., Markham, Ontario, Canada L6C 1Z7

Scholastic Inc.
555 Broadway, New York NY 10012, USA

Scholastic Australia Pty Limited
PO Box 579, Gosford, NSW 2250, Australia

Scholastic New Zealand Ltd.
Private Bag 94407, Greenmount, Auckland, New Zealand

Scholastic Ltd.
Villiers House, Clarendon Avenue, Leamington Spa,
Warwickshire CV32 5PR, UK

The following trademarked names have been used in this book:
Barbie, Beanie Babies

Canadian Cataloguing in Publication Data

McNicoll, Sylvia, 1954-
Caught in a lie

ISBN 0-590-24865-0

I. Title.

PS8575.N52C38 2000   jC813.'54   C00-930823-7
PZ7.M364C38 2000

5 4 3 2 1   Printed in Canada   0 1 2 3 4/0

*For Robin, who's even more beautiful
on the inside.*

*Special applause for the hard-working
men and women in the arts industries
performing difficult tasks in difficult times.
Thank you, Canada Council!*

chapter 1

I'm walking on a runway surrounded by bright-coloured lights — which is my first clue that it's all a dream. For a real fashion show, the lights are white, not this sparkly Christmas red and green. Beyond the sparkles, it's all black, but somehow I know there's an audience hidden there, the kids from my school. My second clue is that I can see myself, the way you only can in dreams. I'm wearing a baby-blue crushed-velvet hip-hugger pantsuit that really highlights my blue eyes, and my cinnamon-coloured hair bounces against my shoulders like in a slow-motion film. I take long strides, my shoulders back and hips pushed forward, my head high and straight — the model walk I've taught myself from fashion television. At the end of the runway now, I stop, turn and smile at the audience. I feel so tall up there, high above those kids for once. And I hear the rush of their applause, I see the flash of more lights — cameras, I think, taking my picture.

Then suddenly the colour drains from the scene and I'm walking down a long hallway carrying a huge stack of files that press against my mouth and nose so that I can hardly breathe. There's a tall grey metal cabinet ahead, the kind my mother has in her office at Halton Board.

The hall seems to grow longer . . . longer . . . as I head towards that cabinet. The lights are bright, the walls and floor bare, like in a hospital . . .

I can feel the panicky nightmare feeling start and I want to pinch myself to wake up, but my hands are full of those stupid folders.

I finally make it to the cabinet, set the files down and take hold of the middle drawer. As I do, I notice some colour on my grey sleeves — embroidered pastel yellow and pink petunias. Ew, they're those awful Wild Spirits petunias, the ones all over the clothes my mother always wears. I'd never own anything with those petunias — this dream is getting worse and worse. I tug at the drawer now, but it's really heavy. I have to brace myself and really pull with both hands.

Finally it slides open and there, in front of me, instead of the usual hanging files, lies a body. This is a morgue, I realize, not Mom's office at all! The eyes of the body are closed, the skin chalk white. A smile is frozen across the face. It's wearing a two-piece hip-hugger outfit. It's . . . me!

"Kimberly, will you come down here and put away your laundry!"

Huh, what? I shake myself and blink. From my

2

bed, I make out the books piled all over my desk. My homework, not all done yet — great.

On the floor, my cue cards lie scattered. Speech day — career speech, even better. It doesn't take a lot to figure out why I had a nightmare. I'd give anything not to have to talk in front of the class.

"Kimberly! Now, please!"

From somewhere behind my eyes a pounding starts. I get up slowly and run a brush through my hair. Usually that relaxes me. Only today my hair snaps and crackles. Static head — bad sign of a big headache on the way — and I'm running late too. I wanted to tackle at least a few more of my algebra equations before I head for school, so Ms Smyrnious doesn't nail me again for not having my homework done. No point now. I can't get the order of operations right when my hair sounds like cereal.

My speech, my speech! It's not ready either. I should go over my cue cards, but there's no time.

In the kitchen, my parents yell back and forth so loud my brain rattles. There's always some dumb problem. All that changes is the argument *du jour*.

"But you promised to pick up the dryer handle *today!*" Mom's voice.

"I've got a lunch meeting." Dad's back at her.

Can't they talk a little softer? My head really hurts. I slink between them towards the laundry room.

"Your clothes are folded on the counter. There's

some whites still in the dryer," my mother calls after me.

I ignore the pile of folded laundry and pry open the dryer with a knife to get at some clean underwear.

The yelling changes into loud talking. "Pick the handle up after work then," Mom counters. She sounds like she's forcing a volume control.

"Can't. Have to meet with Reynolds at five," Dad tosses back.

They are so pathetic. I mean, could they possibly argue about anything more lame? I shake my head as I grab a pair of panties. Uck, the waistband's still damp. I throw them on top of my laundry stack anyway and head back through the kitchen.

"That handle's been on order for three weeks, and now that it's in you can't get it?" Mom again.

"Then it can wait another day," Dad answers.

"What if he sells it to someone else?"

I want to scream, *Can I have some peace and quiet? I have a presentation today!* My head overflows with details for it: *Topic statement first.* And for my algebra: *Multiplication and division before addition and subtraction.* Stupid boring details pushing at the inside of my skull, making the backs of my eyes ache. And now, thanks to them, all that's in my mind is, *Dad better pick up the dryer handle, or else.*

But now Mom turns on me. It looks like peace

4

and quiet isn't going to happen.

"*I've* already made supper for tonight, vacuumed and run a load of laundry . . . and *you're* not even dressed, Kimberly. How long can one person take to get ready?"

I stop and stare at her. She's wearing grey wrinkle-frees and a grey scoop-neck top complete with Wild Spirits petunias — my nightmare come true. Her hair — the same cinnamon tone as mine — is cut in a wash-and-wear do with a row of grey showing at the roots. Her make-up is really hit and miss, and even though she owns contact lenses, she wears out-of-fashion owl frames.

"Some of us should take a little longer," I mutter.

Just my luck, she hears me. "Well, I don't have any time for myself. If someone *else* would do a thing or two around here . . . " And she's off on another rant.

Dad jumps in again to say he *does* do a thing or two around here, such as make the mortgage payments, *blah, blah.* And it becomes the regular ping-pong game. Predictable, boring: "You always . . . You never . . . If only you'd . . . "

With that, I should just quietly sneak away. But instead something comes out of my mouth, almost like the static from my head: my exact thoughts. "I *never* want to be like you!"

chapter 2

Mom's mouth hangs open for one moment — just enough to make my getaway. But the angry words follow: "Teenagers . . . selfish . . . head stuck in those magazines . . . grades would go up . . . bad attitude . . . never get a job."

She doesn't understand. Dull grey housework, rerun arguments, pre-matched petunia fashion, and a boring job. A life like hers — if you can call it a life — would kill me.

Oh . . . *That's* what that dream was really about. *That's* why my body was lying dead in that file drawer. And I'm supposed to study hard and work away on those piles of homework just so I can live like that?

No wonder my hair snaps and crackles and my head aches. Is it really so selfish to want a *real* life? One with excitement and fame, bright colours and stars, and just plain good fashion sense? And one *without* classroom presentations!

I dress very carefully, because even if you don't feel great you should still look your best. Then I gather up my cue cards. Is my speech any good? I squint at the cards. Teachers usually don't like my ideas. Well, okay — I don't like theirs. *Topic statement, supporting details* — the teacher's words throb at the back of my eyeballs. But I'm still supposed to put school first. (My parents' favourite lecture line.) No fun, no fame, no life, unless I do well in school.

It will all be over soon, I tell myself as I sit in my mother's car, damp underwear elastic clammy against my waist. My turn first to give my presentation today. I will unzip my head, dump out all the details on the floor in front of the class. Then the pressure inside my head will ease, the pounding will stop. I'm sure of it. I shut my eyes as Mom drives. When the car stops, I open them again and jump out.

The hall is teeming with bodies that I have to push through. The light seems a little too bright because of my headache. I somehow find my way to class and sit down in my seat. Everyone stands for the national anthem and then sits as the daily announcements drone on. I tune out, and my eyes settle on Ms Smyrnious. What's that I see around her collar? She's wearing a sapphire-coloured shirt. Perfect for her dark hair and skin — she's definitely a Winter. But as I blink again I see, yes, yes! There are three of those awful petunias. That frazzled nightmare feeling floods over me again.

Suddenly it's time. Ms Smyrnious calls me to the front and I get ready to snap myself open and deliver the speech as I walk up the aisle. I stop at a spot a few metres from her desk and then blink a few times, trying to block out the brightness. My head is pounding.

It's hard to make that all-important eye contact when you're blinking like a mole outside its tunnel. But in a few minutes all this agony will be over with if I just concentrate.

"I want to be a model." I lick my lips and try to make out the notes on my cue cards. Wrong order, no good — I shuffle them around, but I can't find the right place so I stash them behind the *Ms Mode* magazine I'm holding. I look up and see Julie at the back of the class. Wow, she had her hair cropped yesterday and it makes her brown eyes seem even bigger. A great look. But we're mad at each other right now — some best friend she is — so I don't even smile. I clear my throat and try again.

"Um . . . um." I knew I shouldn't give the speech right from that first crackle of my hair this morning. But Ms Smyrnious would never understand, and now it's too late. "You told us to back up our career choice? Well, like, this magazine," I hold up my copy, "has a quiz which agrees I'd be perfect in the world of fashion. It's called Ten Ways to Tell if You're Model Material." I flip to page 34. "And here's one of the questions:

How long does it take for you to get ready to go out?

(a) Ten minutes tops. You only wear jeans and Ts and think make-up is unnatural.

(b) Half an hour. You wouldn't be caught dead without blush, lip balm and mascara.

(c) Two hours, because you're worth it. Looking your best is important always."

I stop for a second when Lauren Dreyburgh snickers. She's so unattractive when she laughs. Her nose wrinkles up and her lip rides so high you can see her gums. Doesn't she *ever* look in the mirror and check her smile?

And there's her buddy Stephanie, chuckling along with her. Okay, she's cute — nice high cheekbones — but that red plaid shirt with those boy-cut jeans . . . honestly, why does she dress like a lumberjill? I shake my head and read the last one.

"(d) No time at all. You never go out. Your best friend is the remote."

I raise one eyebrow. Guess we know Lauren and Stephanie are definitely (d)s. I turn back to my page and keep going. "People think you have to be beautiful to be a model, but it says here that regular features and a willingness to work at beauty are more important. Two hours a day on make-up is nothing for a model.

"And I like playing with blush, lip gloss and eye shadow — it's creative. Here's another question:

How fast can you give yourself a new look?
(a) You can't. Your hair and wear are always easy
    and the same."

I pause and make eye contact with Ms Smyrnious again. A mistake. She's frowning. She doesn't
seem to like *Ms Mode* as research backup. I drop
my eyes to those petunias around her neck. They're
enough to make anyone crabby. Now a nice silk
scarf in tangerine . . .

I read the next choice.

"(b) In a weekend. You and your friends do
    makeovers all the time."

I look back at Julie, who's whispering something
to Shelly, one of her new yearbook friends. Julie
and I used to do makeovers all the time till she
joined the yearbook crew. She should give old
Shelly a makeover — some concealer would work
on those zits.

I force my eyes back to the magazine. "Next
choice is:

(c) In an evening. You live by your accessories
    and like fooling around with a curling iron."

Now I just can't help smiling as I glance back up
at Julie — even if we aren't speaking. She's really
the best at accessories. Today I notice she's wearing
brass chains around her neck and both wrists. We
bought those together at the hardware store. Great

against her black turtleneck — a little punk, a little funk. Julie lifts an eyebrow at me and I focus back on the quiz.

"Last choice is:

(d) In a few minutes. You can twist up your hair, throw on a hat or sunglasses and look like a whole different person."

I'm definitely a (d). Getting ready *can* take time, but you have to be able to improvise, too.

"Models have to look different every time the camera shutter opens," I continue reading. "Achieving different looks quickly is extremely important — "

"Kimberly," Ms Smyrnious interrupts.

"Yes, Ms Smyrnious?"

"You're not going to just read the entire quiz, are you? You scored high on it, I presume, so you think you'll suit the job. Is that correct?"

I nod, knowing somehow that won't be enough. So I stammer, "And I think modelling is an exciting job. I won't have to get up every day at the same time, dress in business casual and go to a boring office like my mom and dad."

Ms Smyrnious's face looks as set as those petunias. I have to finish fast now. "And I won't need university for my chosen career, which is perfect, since I think school is a waste of time." *And I won't have to make any more stupid speeches either.* Did I

11

say that out loud? *Just a little joke.* I try a smile out on her, but she doesn't return it. Then I just know I have to wrap it up. "Thank you for listening and I hope you enjoyed my presentation."

From the right side of the room a clapping starts. My boyfriend, Jay, grins, so maybe I did okay. He looks to the left at Matt and then to the right at Carlos, and they clap too. The rest of the class joins in as well. For a moment I'm on the top of that sparkling runway in my dream. Everyone likes me. Jay makes them.

I feel like throwing myself into his arms. Then maybe I can close my eyes and relax. But my head still aches and the clapping sounds too loud now, like spoons banging on pots. It hurts my ears and head.

Ms Smyrnious clears her throat and it stops. "You said you thought school was a waste of time. What about modelling school?"

"That's different." It has to be, doesn't it? I shake my head, and rake my fingers gently through my hair to lift it. "It can't be like *school* school, all boring with x and y junk you never need. I hope it teaches important stuff. Like how to pose for a camera shoot. Different styles for my hair. Things that I like, things that I can be good at."

"Thank you, Kimberly. You may sit down."

I do my model walk back to my seat, but it doesn't feel as good as it did in that dream. Still, I keep a smile on my face. Modelling school? No school at all would be way better. It's one big headache. No modelling classes for me. I want to be discovered.

When I reach my seat I fold my body into it, gracefully. Even with a headache, a model needs to sit down a certain way. Then I open *Ms Mode* and try to close out the world.

Blah, blah, blah, they're all so loud. Andrea, class heavyweight contender and all-around brainer, is up next. She wants to be a veterinarian, a horse doctor. Well, she does have the grace of a large animal with hooves. How fitting. When Carlos whinnies softly Ms Smyrnious doesn't hear, but Andrea stumbles over her words. I'm not the only one who snickers along with the boys. Something about her chubby doll cheeks just inspires that kind of reaction. And when Carlos whinnies a second time, Andrea falls apart and takes off out of the room. It's such a common occurrence Ms Smyrnious doesn't even chase after her. After about one minute of blissful quiet, she just goes on to the next victim, Jay.

Only Jay counted on the presentations taking longer and the speech schedule backing up. Even though he's slotted for today, he's not ready. So Miss-Teacher's-Pal Lauren Dreyburgh volunteers to do her talk a day early. Is she sucking up to Ms Smyrnious or kissing up to Jay? I know she has the hots for him. A blue denim blob, she's wearing her favourite farmer overalls, a trademark *je ne care pas* fashion statement. I find it hard to pay attention to her. What's she saying?

Something hilarious, since the whole class laughs. She's always smart and funny. I look over at Jay. He's laughing too. What a traitor. Does he actually like a smile that shows gums as well as the roots of teeth? Are baggy overalls a big turn-on for him? Honestly, how can he be on Lauren's side?

Everyone's totally relieved when Ms Smyrnious tells us to get out our math texts — there's no time left for any more presentations. I stand my book up in front of me and rest my head on my arms behind it. But Ms Smyrnious won't leave me alone.

"Kimberly, I want you to work this one out on the board." Yuck. Math is bad enough, but stumbling through it in front of everyone . . . Still, she's got a no-nonsense look on her face. "If a model makes 60 dollars an hour for runway work and she pays 20 percent to her agent, how many hours does she need to work to cover her car payment of 528 dollars?"

Let x = number of hours, I write on the board. That's as far as I get. Then I chew on my baby fingernail. Is it because of my headache, or am I seriously confused? I force myself to stop biting my nails. Car payment — wouldn't they just take it out of your bank account? I mean, you'd have extra in there, why would you need to figure it out? It's not like you could say to the fashion designer, "I have enough for my car payment now, see ya."

Ms Smyrnious takes the chalk from my hand. *Bang, bang, bang,* she pounds out the numbers onto the blackboard. "So then you would take 8/10 of 60, or 48 x, which equals 528 . . . *blah, blah, blah, blah, blah.* And the answer is 11 hours." *SCREETCH,* the chalk scrapes out the last number. "Do you understand, Kimberly?"

I nod quickly to make the noise stop. Really, I don't have a clue.

"Now can you see the value of education, no matter what you do for a living?"

Oh . . . *that's* why she picked me — my speech. Get-even time.

"Don't you think you need math even if you become a supermodel?"

Again I nod. I hate all of this. I never get it. My head aches worse; the pain stabs. I want to run out just like Andrea and never come back. But as I sit down, a miracle happens. My *Ms Mode* magazine slips out from underneath my math book and I catch it open on page 35. How can I have missed that? There in bold red letters — my big chance to be discovered and to escape death by boredom: The Great Model Search. I quickly scroll through the tiny print. The deadline's a couple of months away. By the end of June, if things go the way I want them to, I'll never have to face Ms Smyrnious again.

chapter 3

Turning in early is the only thing I can do with a headache like this one. And the next day I feel totally beige inside. (It's not a bad shade to wear with my hair colour, actually, but it's not a great way to feel. Plus my skin turns grey and I need all kinds of toner and blush to perk it up.)

"Kimberly. Get down here now!" Mom calls up the stairs.

I continue outlining my lips with Bruised Berry, my Fashion Five Barbie dolls watching from their shelf. I used to have tons more, but I only kept these to try new looks out on them. There's Evening Barbie. She's wearing an aluminum foil dress I shaped around her, complete with a glued-on sequin trim. Beach Barbie wears a boa bikini made with some feathers pulled from Mom's duster. Wedding Barbie sports a Victorian lace number I improvised from a handkerchief Grams gave me. Casual Barbie wears an old jean pocket I trimmed into a shorts-and-vest set. And Kimberly Barbie's wearing a duplicate of my family studies project, a bandeau for a top and boxers embroidered with her initial. I wish I could try out all those looks on myself, but hey, I don't have the guts to wear aluminum foil to a dance or feathers to the beach.

"You're going to have to walk!" Mom yells.

I fill in my lip lines with Deeply Purple and then stare at my reflection. The light bulbs around it make starry blurs.

Mom won't take off without me because then she'd worry all day about whether I went to school at all. No, she likes to feed me, see me dressed and walking through the school doors, backpack and lunch in hand. Student Barbie. Honestly, Mom just doesn't have a life.

I grin to check for lipstick on my teeth, stand up — unfolding gracefully always — and do a slow turn for my full-length door mirror. No lint on my turtleneck sweater, no sagging hem on my corduroy mini. My textured dark tights look straight, with no snags or runs, and everything goes together well. It takes extra work to look good.

But then I realize in a panic that I'm wearing different shades of grey. Add a petunia trim and I'd be a Mom clone. I need some colour — and not pastels! I snatch up the first thing I see from a hook in my cupboard, a bright plastic necklace made up of large chain links in red, yellow, blue and green. Julie and I nabbed the links from the kindergarten class and snapped them together — they'd been used as math counters by the rugrats. *Finally*

17

math goes to good use. I smile as I link the chain around my neck. Then I hesitate, staring again in the mirror. *Nah, too wild,* I unhook it and hang it back in the cupboard.

"I can't eat," I tell Mom when I finally step into the kitchen. My headaches sometimes leave me feeling like I might throw up. Imagine hurling in public. Nothing's worth that risk.

"Take an apple for the car then. Did you get your homework done? You know if you have trouble with math you can ask Dad."

At the mention of homework my shoulders bunch. I hate when that happens. Deep breath, shoulders back, head up. "I didn't have any trouble," I answer her. That's because I copied Steph's math. I have to say that my numbers were much neater — you can hardly read hers.

As for Dad helping me, he's a computer nerd, not a people person. He can't teach me how to do anything. "There now. That's simple enough, isn't it?" he says when he's finished a problem. But it's not simple to me at all.

Still, all that's not important. In a few months, when I'm on the cover of *Ms Mode,* the x's and y's won't matter.

"Do you have a headache?" Mom stares at me, looking for signs, checking my pupils.

"No," I tell her, which is true by now. Even if I did, I like to save the headache excuse to cut class for special occasions. I stare back at her. She wears a navy print suit with matching earrings, not even one embroidered flower today. Slight improvement, Mom. At least we're both not in grey like some kind of time-warped twins. Although I still wish I could have figured out a way to make my kindergarten necklace work with my look today.

"Take your lunch. And your coat. Do you have your books? Good, let's go." Mom drives me to school like we're way late, and as usual we pull into the parking lot way early. It's freezing out too but that's okay. I see Jay, my sugar puff, near the gate.

"Kimmmberly," Jay calls to me, his breath blowing out in white clouds. He says my name as though it tastes good. "Want to come to Lee's? I need smokes."

From the corner of my eye I notice Andrea standing by herself on the school side of the fence. She's bundled up in a puffy ski jacket and her big blue pop-eyes are staring at me. Her mouth is all scrunched up like a disapproving old granny's. Honestly, she's so gullible. Try and get cigarettes from Lee without ID.

"Sure, I'll pick some up too," I tell Jay, fluttering my eyes to show him I know we're both kidding.

"Smoking's bad for you, Kim. You shouldn't," Andrea nags.

I stop and smile at her. Of course it's bad for you. It yellows your fingers, ages your skin and stinks up your breath. What does she take me for? I might have flunked Grade 4 but Andrea did a second tour of kindergarten. I blow out my cheeks to make fun of her chubby-faced look. "I don't know, Andrea. I just find I *have* to smoke to keep my figure." Then I screw up my face at her and walk away with Jay.

We look good together. He's tall, blond, with good bones and straight teeth, and the only guy I know who knows how to layer properly. He usually wears a shirt over a co-ordinating T. Today he's got one of those jacket vests over a bulky terra cotta sweater — so cute.

I'm just a little shorter but I also have great bones and teeth, important things for print work. Plus my hair has tons of natural body. It's really my best feature when it's not all full of static. "Jay, I need some good pictures of me for this contest I saw in *Ms Mode*. Think you can help me?"

"I'll snap a whole roll tonight. They'll love you. There won't be any contest."

The little bell over the door ding-a-lings as we step into the store. *Only two students at a time*, the sign on the front door reads. Lee could never get away with that if it said *Only two old people at a time*. He and his wife would be the only ones there. Honestly, some people.

I head straight for the magazines, pick up *Teen Fashion* and start flipping. Old Man Lee hates when you read at the rack, so he eyeballs me instead of Jay. Serves him right, then. He should know I always buy the magazine. I feel bubbles of excitement popping through the beige now.

Jay sticks his hands in his pockets and whistles as he checks out the candy bars. Lee's eyes shift to him. Jay grabs a couple, puts one back, then fingers the gum.

"Don't touch unless you buy!" Lee crabs.

I drop my magazine and smile at Lee. "Whoops."

He growls something under his breath.

A suit steps in, snaps up a paper and leaves some change behind. Lee tells him to have a nice day. A lady with a baby pays for some milk and Lee even plays peek-a-boo. Funny how he pretends to like really little kids.

Still Jay browses with his fingers on everything. He never just grabs something quickly. I'm almost screaming inside before he decides. But it's a roller coaster kind of scream. Exciting and scary — I feel way more alive. The beigeness inside me brightens into popsicle pink.

"Dollar seventy-five tax," Lee says when Jay finally plunks down the candy bar. No please or thank you, no smile. And his chocolate bars are double the price of the grocery store's.

Jay grins at him as he hands over the exact change. He's grinning too widely, his eyes sparkling with laughter.

I pay for my magazine and Lee just nods.

"You're welcome," I tell him pointedly. I never rob him. If you ask me, with his prices, *he* robs *us*.

Jay and I stroll from the store back to the school just as the first bell rings. Jay stops in front of the duty teacher, Mrs. Craymore, and turns to face me, smiling as he takes out a pin with a tiny brown bear carrying a little red heart. It's the Children's Hospital Charity Bear, and he's so adorable.

Charity Bear, hmm. Stealing from Lee seems only fair to me, but from the Children's Hospital, well, the people there were really nice to me when I went there for my headaches. I personally didn't take it, though, and what kind of loser would turn a present down when it's already been stolen anyhow? I'll throw some money in the jar next time I visit Lee's.

Besides, I want Lauren Dreyburgh to see my little bear. Maybe she'll understand then. Sure Jay laughs at her dumb cracks. She's way smarter than me too. But it's *me* he wants to be seen with, and *me* he gives a charity bear to.

Jay pins it on my collar and I know he wants to kiss me. Not like I'd let him. Not at school — it doesn't look good. Plus I like to make him wait. It's part of my plan from 31 Tips to Make Your Hottie Pant in last month's *Teen Fashion*.

Mrs. Craymore gives a little cough. "Shouldn't you be getting to class now?"

"Yes, Mrs. Crayyy-more," we say together and drift inside only as the second bell rings.

In language arts, horsy Andrea tries her presentation again. Perfect. If everyone does their speech twice we'll be spared doing one of Ms Smyrnious's famous novel studies. I hate reading the books she gives us but what's worse are the activities that go along with them. They're so much work! Last time we had to write a diary for a girl who lived a hundred years ago. Ms Smyrnious complained I didn't get into the historical details or the character's emotions enough. Instead I talked about the fashion implications — how cool it must have been to sew your own clothes, picking the fabrics and styles rather than buying off the rack. Aren't those historical facts too? Okay, so the pioneer crowd *was* pretty much stuck with cottons and wools and they had to wash their stuff by hand. I was trying to accentuate the positive. Anyway, just because Ms Smyrnious doesn't get emotional about clothes and fashion doesn't mean a girl a hundred years ago couldn't. That's what I mean by teachers never liking my ideas.

Andrea's lip trembles and she stares down at her hand where's she's obviously written her notes this time. I can't stand it. She's so pathetic I just have to tune out. Instead of listening, I look over the *Teen Fashion* I bought from Lee's, relax and fold over the corner at Five Beauty Tips You Probably Don't Know. I'll try them out later. Before Jay takes my picture.

Then I read about kids' most embarrassing moments. Four stars are the ultimate hide-under-a-rock humiliations; three means you still blush when you think about it; two, your buds still laugh about it; one, you wish it had happened to someone else. Most of them have to do with bodily noises and periods — ugh, so gross. Some are about mega-zits appearing or exploding at the wrong time, others are about straps breaking or pants splitting, and a few are about being caught spreading gossip or telling a lie.

I like reading them and feeling smarter than all those kids. Nerds like Andrea handle school well, but I'm good at real life. Which is why I check my teeth and clothes in the mirror every morning — food doesn't need to hang from your teeth, you can catch the embarrassing stains yourself, and clothing won't give out on you in front of everybody. If Andrea looked in the mirror every day, she would never let herself eat so much. As far as zits and all that other body stuff, well I eat right and drink lots of water. None of that stuff ever happens to me.

Time to tick off Andrea's evaluation sheets. I give her top marks for everything — A+. Hey, I can be generous when she's not being Miss All-Perfect-Student. I drift through the other presentations the same way, reading ads and checking out fashions in the magazine. It's pretty much all I can handle the rest of the day while I have the after-headache beige brains.

At home after school, I check page 35 of *Ms Mode* again and try to focus. They want a clear colour snapshot, which is why I need Jay, and fifty words about why I think I should be considered for their Great Model Search.

> I love clothes and make-up. I've been dressing up Barbies since I was three. I still like making outfits for them.

Does that sound too babyish? The girl they choose will travel the world, and they can't have some kid who still plays with dolls. I start again.

> I love fashion and make-up and have been designing and sewing clothes since I was ten.

A little whitish lie never hurt.

> I have studied models and modelling for a couple of years now. And while I enjoy working hard on beauty, I do have even skin tones and my best feature is my hair. I hope you will book an appointment for me when you are in Hamilton.

> Yours sincerely,
> Kimberly Rainer

The writing is blah, I know. It's a schooly kind of thing, not what I'm good at. I stare at my entry for a minute. How important can writing be anyway, when they're splashing your face all over their magazine? A picture's worth a thousand words, right?

The photograph will have to sell them on me, I decide. *Come on and call me, Jay.* And if his snapshot shows the real me, there won't be any problem.

chapter 4

A watched telephone never rings. So I pick up *Teen Fashion* and flip to this month's quiz: The Best Kind of Best Bud — How to Tell if You Are One.

This is kind of a toughie for me because of my tiff with Julie. I pick up the large picture frame Julie gave me for my last birthday. It has one big slot and six smaller slots around it. Julie slipped a school picture of her in one of the small slots and one of Jay in another. In the large slot is my favourite picture of me, a glamour shot taken last year as a birthday present from Mom. The other four slots are filled with clippings of my fave models, Jan Johannsen and Lianne Ulan. I can't help thinking I look just as good as Jan and Lianne.

I stare at Julie. Great brown eyes and long lashes. She's cute and smart, but she's always browsing my room like a kid in a museum, her hands all over the place. *It's your fault,* I tell her picture, and set the frame back down on my bureau. Still, I miss her.

But I like to do quizzes, so I use Jay as my best friend. I grab a pen off my desk, ready to check off my choices.

Your best friend forever tells you a major secret. You:

(a) only tell one other person and make them promise not to say anything to anyone.
(b) put it in the school newspaper next time you're mad at her.
(c) try to forget the secret so you don't blab.

Jay doesn't talk to me about really personal stuff, but I know plenty about him that's not public knowledge. His dad's a principal at Mapleview High down the block a ways — I know Jay likes to keep that quiet. His parents sleep in separate bedrooms. I only found that out because Jay's room is really the master bedroom — huge, with its own bathroom. Jay swiped the track balls from all the mice in the computer labs so we could play pitch and catch back in Grade 5. That was a really hard one to keep secret — the whole class was supposed to have to stay after school till someone confessed, and the teacher kept staring at me. I thought something on my face would show. I'm a point-earning (c) on this one.

You just bought the perfect tank top, your BFF begs to borrow it to impress a new crush on a first date. You:

(a) simply never lend personal articles of clothing. It's not hygienic.
(b) lend it to her in exchange for that hot new mini she wears.
(c) hand it to her with a smile. What's yours is hers.

This is where I got into the fight with Julie. I had just bought these great lavender-coloured suede boots with my grandmother's Christmas money. They went right up to my knee and they looked so funky with this violet-coloured skirt I had. She wanted to borrow them. I know I'm going to lose points for picking (a), but it's true. I don't want Julie's feet in my shoes or her body in any of my clothes.

Your BFF returns the formerly perfect tank top, but there's a big stain right on the front. You:

(a) say nothing and spray some Outspot on it, hoping for the best.

(b) give her the bill. It was brand new, after all.

(c) return her hot new mini in doll size. Oops, weren't you supposed to machine wash it in hot water?

Well, wrecking my tank top is exactly the kind of thing Julie would do. She's all energy and speed, like a tornado, grabbing things, knocking them over, spilling stuff. But I check off (a). I would say nothing. I'm still saying nothing to her after she pulled off Beach Barbie's arm last week. What's the point? It's what Julie does. I can never make her understand about the Barbies especially — she just thinks I'm weird. So instead, I usually just clear a path for Julie. And she didn't notice I was mad anyway, until I refused to lend her the boots.

What's the next question?

No time to do a major homework assignment, so your BFF wants to borrow your homework. You:

(a) hand it over. Some day she'll do the same.
(b) offer to help her at lunch instead. After all, copying is cheating.
(c) tell her you didn't have time yourself. What makes her assume you did, anyway?

This one makes me cringe. Jay wanted my history notes the other day but I honestly didn't have any. I was thinking of something else when Ms Smyrnious was talking. And Julie, well, she's always lending me her homework, but if I'm really honest, (c) would be my answer. Only what I told her would be the truth, and the magazine doesn't let you have any extra points for that.

A major hottie asks you out when you promised your best friend you'd go to the Dozers concert with her. You:

(a) fake a bad cough when you tell her over the phone you're running a fever and your mom won't let you go.
(b) suggest another night to your new boytoy. Boyfriends come and go but best friends are forever.
(c) buy another ticket to the concert for your hottie. The more the merrier.

Imagine buying an extra ticket for another boy when you're already going to a concert with a best friend who's a boy. Jay.

I have to choose (a) if I'm really being honest,

even though it's obvious (b) is the right answer.

The whole quiz doesn't work out, and I'm not surprised that when I add all my score, I end up in the wrong category: Loner.

> A loner, you're too into doing your own thing to share your time or your things with a best bud. Remember, though, exciting things become even more exciting when you have someone you care about to experience them with.

I wonder about that for a moment. Besides just making me feel good about myself and cheering me up, Jay for sure pumps up the excitement level in my life. And Julie? Tornado Girl's a great person to shop with, she has a good fashion eye and she always has terrific ideas. Although sometimes I think I'm not brainy enough for her. She's always hanging around with the browner yearbook crew. And so far she doesn't even seem to miss me.

Hmph! She'll be sorry once I win the Great Model Search. Then she'll come crawling back. Even her yearbookies will want to be my friend. I toss the magazine aside.

Why isn't Jay calling? I hate phoning first, but I hate waiting too. Should I change into a less preppy outfit or not? Put on fresh make-up?

I dial his number but his little sister Brianne answers.

"Jay can't come to the phone. He's cut off and grounded for a month."

"But I can't wait that long! Can't he talk for just a second? I need him. What if I just show up over there?"

"Ooo! I don't think so. He'll tell you all about it at school tomorrow."

"Great," I snap as I hang up the phone. "Great, great, great," I yell as I throw myself onto my bed. What did he do *this* time? Why does he get himself caught, doing whatever it was, when he knows I need his help with this contest?

chapter 5

"Don't be mad. C'mon. It's not my fault. Wait till you hear what I did."

Giving Jay The Treatment is hard when his ears look all red and cold and his eyes all watery blue. I lean back against the school fence, the wind blowing against my face, and I reach up to pat my hair in place. Then I just shake my head instead so that the wind will lift and billow it back. "Did you bring a camera?"

Jay's face scrunches and he slaps his forehead with the heel of his hand.

I click my tongue at him and turn my face away. "You could have taken the pictures at lunch."

"Tomorrow, I swear." Jay lifts one hand stop-sign style and puts the other over his heart.

I roll my eyes and ignore him for a second longer till I notice Lauren and her scrawny best friend Stephanie heading up the blacktop. Lauren looks with round love-eyes at Jay, but she can't have him, he's mine. So I turn back to face him and give him a bright understanding smile. "Oh all right, Jay, what did you do this time?"

Taking my books from my locker, I can hear all the buzz on Jay.

"It's only because his father's a principal. Otherwise he'd be suspended." Carlos sounds as if he's bragging.

"How did he log onto the teacher chat line without a password?" Emily asks.

Carlos shakes his head. "Got his father's, I guess. The great thing is that Ms Norr actually believed he *was* Mr. Farber. She even agreed to go to the movies with him."

I slam my locker shut. Serves Norr right. She's always hauling Jay into her office, lecturing him about his attitude. And what does she write at the bottom of my progress report? "Needs remedial help." I had to beg my father not to enrol me in Can-do Math. Still, a no-show date with Mr. Farber . . . I shudder and then laugh. Jay has one amazing sense of humour.

"Get in on any interesting chat rooms lately, Kim?" Matt asks me, grinning.

"Who me?" I wrinkle my nose and shake my head. "I'm more of a cellphone person." Then I toss my hair back and walk into the classroom, just making it to my seat as Julie stands up. She has to give her presentation first thing. Gosh, that new haircut's *great* on her. I touch my shoulder and tug at one of my curls. I'd love to try that length, but it's an awful risk.

Julie smiles at Ms Smyrnious. "I'd like to be a photo journalist."

She's wearing black leather cargo pants with a brown cashmere sweater the same shade as her eyes. Around her neck she's snapped our kindergarten find — only she's taken out the red and blue links. She's left with a cute choker made up of yellow and green. *That's* what I should have done the other day, except with my outfit I would have kept the red and blue. Julie has guts, and she's the only other person with a lick of fashion savvy in this class — or maybe even the school.

If only she hadn't roughhoused my Barbie. I know that I'm too touchy about my Fashion Five, and that a loose doll arm shouldn't be such a big deal. It just didn't put me in the mood to lend her my suede boots . . . like anything could. And everything broke down from there.

" . . . It would be great to travel the world and illuminate the problems of the homeless and diseased through photos. I'll probably have to start by taking pictures of weddings, graduations . . . "

I glance at my magazine. Why didn't I think of Julie first? She can take my picture for the Great Model Search! With that professional-quality camera and all those fancy lenses she has . . . I'll have to talk to her at lunch. She'll want to do this for me, I know it. And in return I certainly don't mind lending her my lavender suede boots now. They have a stain on them anyway — how much more can she wreck them? And Beach Barbie's arm snapped back on. The world is so much clearer to me when I've had a good night's sleep and my head's not pounding.

Jay finally gives his talk on how he wants to design computer games when he grows up.

"Maybe a computer *dating* game," Matt cracks. Ms Smyrnious makes him sit in the back with her, so there are no more laughs from then on. I give Jay A+ and a perfect score for everything. At least he's into games, not the kind of stuff Dad does at all, so it's not major geekville.

Math goes okay too, because even Ms Smyrnious is impressed with my neatness. Ten out of ten I get. I didn't copy the bonus question from Stephanie's work. That's where being smart about life comes in. Smyrnious would have been too suspicious.

"What a great colour that is for you, Julie," I say as I pull up a chair at her lunch table. I hate apologies, myself. Compliments are way better.

Her yearbook friends pack up and head off for important activities the minute I sit. But Julie stays and that's a good sign.

Her eyes widen and her eyebrows lift. For another moment it looks like she won't talk to me.

I lift my eyebrows too, tilt my head and shrug one shoulder, smiling out a sorry. Is she going to make me say it out loud?

Finally she smiles back. "Thanks." She narrows her eyes again. "I'm not sure about the necklace . . . " She fiddles with the links around her neck.

"It introduces a new colour." I nod. "But you took a risk and I really admire that about you." *Just not when you take risks with my things.*

"Thanks, Kim." She pats the necklace now. "Coming from you, that means a lot."

"And your talk today was really good. I didn't realize how serious you've become about photography. I just thought you liked hanging around with the yearbook gang. But travelling and making a statement about world conditions does sound exciting." I stop and take a breath. "So listen. I have this really great idea."

Julie leans forward in her chair. "What?"

"You could do me a big favour and I think it could work really nicely for you." I explain about my contest and how I will credit each photo with her name. "Once a model becomes famous, they dredge up every picture available and then, you see, they'd publish the pictures you took along with your photo credit. You'd have your first break into the world of photo journalism."

Julie's hooked. We put Barbie and the suede boots behind us and it's great to be friends again. The rest of the lunch hour we pore over fashion magazines. She comments on poses and lighting, I pick out style and accessory pointers. Then she quizzes me from a special Love Edition of *Ms Mode*: How to Tell if Your Boytoy is Loveworthy.

It's funny because every once in a while when I look Jay's way, I catch him watching me. But it's a good thing to deprive him today. That'll teach him to let me down when I need him. I have to keep making him chase me so he doesn't let Lauren get her mitts on him. A little hard-to-get is always good, according to 31 Ways to Make Your Hottie Pant.

Julie nudges me. "Answer the question, c'mon, Kim. When you spend time with him do you feel: (a) excited and nervous, (b) supercomfortable, (c) pretty and smart. Just choose one."

I stare at the page. "But it's stupid: (b) and (c) are the same for me, really. All right, (c) then."

Julie adds up my score and it turns out Jay is a Pal with Promise, the highest category, which in turn means we can enter the Love Zone sometime. But with Jay grounded for a month and no camera . . . Staring at me or not, Jay will definitely not be entering the Love Zone today.

After school, I go over to Julie's, anxious to get started on the photos right away. We usually go to my house, but today we need her camera. I follow her up to her room. It's been a while and I've forgotten how strange it is.

"Wow, these new posters, they're so . . . " Depressing, I want to say. But I catch myself. I just barely got Julie back — I don't want to go and ruin it now, especially not before the photo shoot. "Black-and-white. They're new, aren't they?"

Julie nods and smiles. "The work of Charles Harsh — I did a project on him for art."

I smile back. "Have you seen the photos that are all black-and-white with just some accent pieces in red or yellow?"

"Yeah, but what could Harsh accent in the shot of the starving Ethiopian child?" Julie flounces onto her unmade bed. Yuck. I make my bed every day so that my room looks good.

"Nothing, I guess. But in the shot of that man dying of AIDS? He could add a yellow rose to his bedside. Or, I know — What colour is the AIDS awareness ribbon?"

"Red."

"They could put a red ribbon on his pyjamas. That's it. Like your choker, a little splash of colour."

"But it would be like advertising, wouldn't it?" Julie looks thoughtful. She isn't mad at me, which is good — I haven't said the wrong thing. "He's not trying to sell red ribbons."

"What do I know?" I go to sit on the corner of her desk, but see the layer of dust there. "Maybe we should go to my house for the actual pictures. I mean, I need to change, to have different looks."

Julie begins snapping pictures. "I'll finish this

roll of film today. Tomorrow we'll do the full-fledged cover-girl thing. Now, think of something sad," she tells me.

I think of my mother and father rushing off to their drudgy office jobs, always looking tired and disappointed. I'd do anything not to end up like them. I can't imagine anything more sad than a life like that.

Julie clicks quickly.

"Something angry."

Ms Smyrnious failing me in math and language arts and on that history project! *Click, click.*

"Exciting."

Picture taking, actually doing something about my future, remembering about Jay slipping candy bars right from underneath Lee's nose — all of them make bubbles of excitement form inside me. I toss my hair wildly. I'll never be like my parents. Hurray! *Click, click, click.*

"Something happy."

Me wearing a designer gown with elegant accessories. Everyone watching and applauding. *Click, click, click, click.*

"That's great. I'll develop these at school tomorrow." Julie winds her camera, then opens the back, takes out the film and pops it into a tube.

"Thanks, Julie." I unsnap the buckle on my backpack. "Do you mind looking at my entry. Just to see if my wording is okay?" I pull out the blue piece of paper I used to write my fifty words.

Julie takes it and reads for a few seconds, frowning. "Don't take this the wrong way or anything."

"It's stupid, right?" I pull back the piece of paper.

"No, the entry's fine, really. And I think you'd make a great model. But why just rely on this contest?"

I pick off some lint from my skirt. "What do you mean?"

"Well, photographers hang from airplanes, sneak into parties, chase limos — anything to get their shot. If you want to be a model, you should do more than just wait to win a contest. You should try a real modelling agency. Maybe you'll even get some experience before this contest."

"Dad would never let me. Not with my grades and all."

"Does he really have to know? I mean, I didn't tell my mom about climbing the railway bridge when I took the photo of the eagle's nest."

The bubbles of excitement pop inside me then. I remember why I like Julie, all over again. "You're right. Dad really doesn't have to know." I sit down on her bed. What's a little dust or lint on my skirt? It's washable. "So how do you think I should do it?"

chapter 6

Ms Ferris checks out our boxer shorts next day in family studies. It's the extra easy beginner sewing project for super-morons. She'd decided it was cheaper to buy a kit so we basically got to choose the size and colour of plaid and that was it. Bor-ing.

I sewed mine in green, and just for fun, cut out little square slits on the legs. These I folded over and double stitched and when I still had extra time, I drew on a black K and machine embroidered it.

Ms Ferris fingers the K and frowns. Then she studies the slits and the elastic waistband. "You have a nice eye for detail, Kimberly. You could do well in design."

I shrug my shoulders. It's really no biggie. I go into this other world when I'm creating clothes — time means nothing. I don't mind matching up plaid, stitching evenly and adding little touches. It's actually a disappointment when I'm done suddenly and just snap back into the grey school world again. I glance over Lauren and Stephanie's shorts. Red plaid, blue plaid, crooked seams and lopsided.

"We don't have that long till the end of the term.

But if you're willing to put in extra time, perhaps your next project could be more challenging. Here you go." The slip of paper Ms Ferris hands me has my grade on — A+.

I can't help smiling. The first A+ of my life. Do models need detail for their work? It can't hurt. But it won't help much with my parents. "That's nice, dear," my dad will say with a smile. What he really cares about is courses that lead to university. My A+ won't convince him that I can apply to a modelling agency and keep my grades up.

Jay hands Ms Ferris misshapen red plaid boxers with long black threads dangling from the seams.

"Why didn't you use matching thread?" Ms Ferris turns her head on an angle.

"I lost mine. Carlos lent me his." Jay's blue eyes plead with her.

"You should have clipped the thread as you went along. It's much easier and less messy afterwards."

"I forgot." Jay grins, and his face turns a winning shade of pink. "I'll trim them now."

"Very well, here's your grade." She hands him a slip of paper, guaranteed not to be the F he deserves, since he never sewed anything at all. He swiped someone's scrapped project from the wastepaper basket yesterday. He gives me a thumbs up and makes a C with his other hand.

I wink back at him.

It might have been a perfect day. But next period Smyrnious announces the stupid math test she's giving. It will cover everything from multiples to fractions and count for thirty percent of our final grade.

We have a whole month to get ready, she tells us cheerily. So we have plenty of opportunity to see her if we need help. Sure. Does anybody really like to hang back and spend extra time with the teacher? My shoulders bunch up, my neck stiffens. I catch myself with my fingers close to my mouth, my teeth ready to grind onto my nails.

"Never mind math. I'll take you out to lunch to celebrate my pass in family studies," Jay tells me.

Lunch away from school is just what I need. I grab his arm. "But we have to be back on time. I can't get in trouble this week, Jay. I need some space for my modelling thing."

"Camera!" He smacks his forehead. "I forgot it again, sorry."

"Don't worry, Julie is taking my pictures. But I was supposed to eat with her today." I look back to see her heading for the cafeteria with Shelly. I wave and try to catch her eye but they both ignore me. Obviously she doesn't care if I go to lunch with her or not. "Aw, you can take me to lunch. I'll see her after school anyway."

We head out the door together. At the next corner he stops at the strip mall bank. "Just need some money. It'll only take a minute." He waves a baby blue bankbook with a bicycle at me. I recognize it as the boy equivalent of the My First Bankbook I have at home, the one my parents deposit grandparent and birthday money into.

I wait to the side as he hands a withdrawal slip to the teller. She talks to him for a moment and he whips out his wallet, showing her a student ID card. Then she counts out a lot of bills.

Jay positively bounces from the bank, he seems so happy. But there's an icy hard glitter to his eyes that I don't understand. "That'll show my father," he tells me. He holds up a wad of bills. "Grounded a month for a little joke. Overkill or what!" He pockets the cash and takes hold of my hand. "It's my money anyway and I'm not going to McGill!"

I understand just how Jay feels. My dad graduated from Western and is on at me all the time how I should go. Another four years of school, sure. I wish I could make my father understand what I want. *I have an eye for detail, Dad. A flair for fashion and great colour sense.* But things *I* like don't interest him.

Jay and I share a pizza at Luciano's, a preppy little Italian restaurant with checkered tablecloths and takeout. Jay orders vegetarian just for me and he even pays extra for artichokes. He tips well and I feel proud of him.

On our way out he pockets almost the whole bowl of mints.

"No thank you," I tell him when he offers me some. "I don't eat unwrapped candy."

Then Jay stuffs the whole handful into his mouth and his cheeks bulge out with little lumps. I have to laugh. My neck doesn't feel all stiff anymore and my shoulders unbunch. It's like something heavy has been lifted off. I touch my little charity bear and don't think about math the rest of the day.

After school Julie walks home with me. It's a long walk but it beats hanging around school till Mom can pick me up. Julie acts all quiet for a while, and I figure maybe she's mad about me blowing off our lunch date.

"Look, you didn't really wait for me for lunch — you know you didn't. I called for you but you were talking to Shelly." Julie rolls her eyes and now I know that's what she's mad about. "Listen, I just had to get away from school today and Jay asked me out." I turn to her. "I should have chased after you to let you know. I . . . I'm sorry."

She nods. Funny, she has all her yearbook friends to sit with, and yet she missed me. Hmm. I smile. By the time we get home she seems fine anyway. After we each eat a fruit cocktail yogurt we head for my room. Julie immediately flicks on my mirror lights and stares at herself for a few seconds. Then she grabs Kimberly Barbie from my shelf. I cringe.

"Her outfit's exactly like your family study box-ers. That's so cute. Mother and daughter," Julie says. "Did you embroider that B on the shorts?"

I nod.

"You are amazing. I love the bandeau." She fin-gers the folded piece of fabric that I'd used as a kind of bikini top on the doll.

"It's just a twist of fabric with a couple of stit-ches." Anybody can do this stuff.

I want to scream when she yanks Kimberly Barbie's hair back to look at the little ruffle I've also sewn. She's just so rough.

"Hey, you should make yourself a hair accessory like this," she says as she pulls the hair in a differ-ent direction. "Then you could use it to put your hair up. I bet you it would look great."

"Gently!" I warn and then check myself. "Here, let me put Barbie's hair up." I calmly take the doll from Julie's hand, twist Barbie's ponytail into a quick topknot and then place her back on the shelf. Not something I would chance on my own head.

"So did you call yet?" Julie asks when she sees the big telephone book on my desk.

I shake my head. "I didn't know which one to try. I didn't know . . . " I can't tell her I felt scared. What if they said no? What if they didn't like cinnamon-coloured hair? What if they wanted girls who could make people laugh, or multiply x's. What if they just plain hated me? What would be left for me then? I couldn't bear thinking that I actually might be forced to file folders someday or stare at a computer screen.

Julie leafs through the Yellow Pages and sticks her finger on an ad. "This one. Chevron. I heard they're really good. Do you remember Rebecca from last year?"

"The tall girl that moved away at Christmas?" I ask.

"Yeah. She's at my cousin's school now. Anyway, My cousin says Rebecca models with Chevron all the time. She was in all the Patches flyers, and you're ten times as good looking as she is."

Patches, my favourite store. I'd love to be in their flyer. "What will I say if they answer? I'm no good at talking. I can't do it."

"This is a practice for your big contest. C'mon, Kim."

I hold out the portable phone. "You do it, Julie. Pretend to be my mother and call. Please?"

She takes it and keys in the numbers. "You're such a big chicken, Kimberly." She holds up a hand. "Uh, yes. My name is Mrs. Rainer. I would like your agency to represent my daughter." Julie puts on an English accent as she speaks. "Colour or black-and-white? Uh huh. Absolutely, we'd love to come in for an interview. Wait a minute, April twenty-third is no good for me. That date is a shareholder's meeting. Oh no, she can manage on her own. How be I dash her off a note and she gets there on the bus? She's only fourteen but everyone says she looks eighteen. And she is very mature. You like that in your models, don't you?"

Apparently they do. I feel a little uncomfortable with her doing Mom, but the bubbly excitement popping inside me is worth it. Julie hangs up the phone. "She has open call day next month, the second-last Wednesday, from two till six," she tells me and we high five.

"Thanks, Julie. I'll never forget this. Come on, sit down." I pat the chair in front of my make-up mirror and pull out my magazine. "I'm going to try these five hot beauty tips out on you first!" I want to do something really nice for Julie. "Why are you laughing?"

Julie points to my new make-up kit. "You bought a fishing tackle box to keep that stuff in!"

"It's called a Vanity Organizer and it was on special last week, thank you very much. These are the tools of the trade and I like them in order." I frown at her. Then I read the first tip. "Outline the lips in the same shade of lipliner as the lipstick. This will create fuller looking lips."

I sort through my pencils, searching for just the right one. "Oh, this will be great for you!" Julie's top lip stretches pencil thin across her face. I push up my sleeves and then outline her lips slowly, concentrating, with my mouth slightly open to steady my hand. "Perfect." The new lip line rests just at the edge of her natural lips. I also dot and x some liner on her lip itself for "more lasting colour." "What do you think?"

"A little clownish, I'd say. Don't you think?" She turns to me.

I think that some people have no taste, but I smile and tell her, "No, it's an improvement." Next I read about using foundation around the eyes as well as the rest of the face to provide a better base for eye make-up. I dab on the perfect shade of liquid over Julie's skin. I also dot on the black eyeliner and blend it as they suggest. After brushing Midnight Mocha mascara on her lashes, I comb them out to declump them.

The final tip, which I've known practically since kindergarten, is to "apply blush with an upwards stroke from the hollow in the cheek across the outer edge of the cheekbone." And for Julie, the colour has to be . . . Roseberry, I decide after searching through my box. What do I expect from all this work? Just a little gratitude, maybe even some awe at my talent with makeovers.

I stand back. "You look fabulous." And then it hits me. Fabulous enough to enter the contest herself. I chew at my thumbnail.

"I don't know," she says as she stares at her reflection. "It's not really me."

Of course not, it's way better. I stop chewing and

take a deep breath. "You weren't thinking about entering, yourself, were you?"

Julie laughs. "C'mon, you know modelling's not my thing."

I smile at her. "Of course. It's just you look sooo good." She could never beat me out anyway, I'm pretty sure. Still I breathe easier and feel happier.

"Okay, now it's my turn to do you," she says, turning to stand up.

"That's okay. I can do it faster myself." I sit down at the table and pull the box towards me. "Why don't you check out my closet and see which outfit you think would look good in the shots."

I even try a new shade of lipstick, I feel so good. And I like the effects of the five hot beauty tips on my own face. I turn one way, then the other. Good bones — they have to pick me. I smile. Great teeth. How can they not pick me? I stretch my neck. Perfect posture. I look over at Julie. It all depended on her pictures. They better pick me.

"How about wearing the boxers you made in family studies, along with a matching T-shirt? That way you can adjust your fifty words to say you designed and sewed the outfit in the picture?"

"You think they'd be impressed with a family studies project?" I wrinkle my nose. "Still, it's kind of different."

"They'll show a lot of leg. Models need to look leggy," Julie tells me. "And let me show you what I dug up at the library last night." She reaches into her backpack and takes out an old *Ms Mode*. "Last year's winner and runners up." She flips open the magazine.

"Let me see that." I grab it from her hands. Boy, that Julie . . . Who would have ever thought of doing research on the contest entries? I flip open the magazine to the right spot quickly. Last year's winner was fifteen-year-old Lynne Marie Rightcort. "Look at how skinny her eyes are! I can't believe she won."

Julie points. "Never mind. Look at what she's wearing!"

"You're right, her dress is really short."

"Check out first runner-up." Julie flips the page.

"What a big nose. It's a banana, I swear." Julie and I laugh.

"Look at this one, her eyelids are bald." Julie stabs the page with her finger, in hysterics now.

"Bet she doesn't unclump her eyelashes," I join in, realizing again how much I've missed having Julie as a friend.

I also let her snap a whole roll of me in the boxers.

"Oh my gosh, I forgot to show you yesterday's pictures," Julie says as she tucks her camera away. She fishes for an envelope and slips out a pile of snapshots. "The school lab only does black-and-white, but I think you'll like them."

The stark dark shots suck my breath away. "But the contest asked for colour."

"That's okay. I'll drop the next rolls off at Economart. They'll be exactly what you want. Not like these, of course."

I start shuffling through the pictures in horror. "My mouth is open too wide here . . . I look like a hyena in this one. . . That shadow looks like a scar . . . " I start to breathe more quickly. How can this happen? I don't look like any of these. Yet they'd be perfect for one of Julie's depressing posters. And I need to win that contest. "Julie, these are awful!"

"They're prize-winning photographs. You just don't understand what to look for." Julie's mouth turns down unattractively.

I try to save the day again. "I'm sure they are. And you can use them for a photo contest if you like. But for the model search, I'd like to look more . . . well . . . like that." I point to my glamour shot in the frame she'd given me.

"Why don't you just use that one, then?" Julie complains.

"Because I'm so much more mature now and because I know you can take a better picture. Please? Could you try? Can you shoot lots of rolls?"

Julie shakes her head at me. "Fine, I'll keep taking pictures till you find a photo you like. It's good practice anyway."

So I quickly switch to a more formal look, a blue silkette mini dress. Blue is a sincere colour — I think — and with my gold locket, I figure I look sophisticated enough to represent *Ms Mode* around the world. I only hope the magazine does too.

chapter 7

"Here they are, your last-chance photos." Julie makes a face as she slaps some thick envelopes onto the table. "There's no time to have any more pictures developed before your Chevron appointment today."

"You know what they say, Tenth time's a charm. Thanks!" I push my salad aside to make room and my hands tremble as I reach for one.

"Tenth! More like the seventeenth, Kim. You better find one you like there."

"And I appreciate your patience," I tell her as I flip through. My eyes are closed in the first one. In the next three they're red as rabbits'. Picture after picture looks awful — as usual — each for a different reason. My neck stiffens as I shuffle through the stack. That can't be what I look like, I think. But it's been the same story for every roll Julie's taken over the past four weeks. "My hair looks so . . . muddy-coloured," I complain as I nibble at the nail on my index finger.

"That's the developing, not me," Julie says. "And there's nothing wrong with brown." Her smile straightens.

Emily, one of Julie's friends, rushes over and sits down. "Did you notice Andrea today? She lost some weight and she's starting to look good."

My salad fork snaps. "Oh pul-lease," I say, looking up for a moment and rolling my eyes. Then I concentrate on the pictures again. "The skin under my chin is bunchy in this one." What's wrong with stupid Julie? She's supposed to be good at photography. Why can't she take one decent picture of me!

Jay slams his books down on the table and heads towards the cafeteria line. "Wow, Andrea's hot," he whispers loudly as his head swivels to follow her.

I roll my eyes at him. It's not the first time he's said that since Andrea started losing weight, but I'm sick of hearing it. "Have some class," I hiss in his ear as I go over to get a new fork for my salad.

"Andrea looks great, don't you think?" I overhear Lauren asking her best buddy Stephanie.

"Andrea this, Andrea that," I mutter, still feeling rotten about Julie's seventeenth roll of Ugly Shots. Okay, so Andrea's not a porker anymore, but still, all this attention she's getting is really overdone. Nobody tells you your figure's great when it's always been that way.

I head back to our table and throw the fork down next to my salad. Then I sit down and shuffle on to the next photo. "Look at the expression on my face. I look like a witch."

"Look like one?" Emily says.

Who asked her to sit with us anyway? I raise my eyebrows and curl a lip. "You're just not funny, Emily."

"More pictures," Jay interrupts as he places his tray on the table. "Who's the babe?" He grins as he picks up a shot of me in my boxer shorts.

Even if he was on Andrea's cheerleading team, it's hard to stay mad at Jay. "Do you really like that one?" I take the picture back from him. Maybe he's right. "My ears look okay? Honestly, I mean?"

"What ears?" Jay says. "Can I have it?

"No." I put the print to the side just in case it turns out to be the best of the worst. "First we have to see which ones I'm using tonight and which one I'm mailing to the model search."

"All those other ones weren't any good?" Jay asks as he bites into his hamburger.

"You got it!" I wrinkle my nose as I pull out another shot and pat his back. "Are my ears really that big?"

"Your ears are big, your neck bunches and in certain lights, your hair is brown," Julie snarls at me. "Still, with all those pictures you should find one where all that doesn't show. Here, what's wrong with this one?" Julie holds out a shot where my ears are covered, my head up and my mouth straight except for a tiny upwards curl on one lip.

"I look smug," I complain. I don't like the girl in the picture.

"What are you talking about? It looks just like you," Jay says, still chomping away.

I roll my eyes and slap it to one side just in case.

"Where is it you're going today again?" Jay asks.

"She's *only* meeting Elaine Chev of the Chevron Modelling Agency." Julie explains this in a tone that says there's nothing "only" about the open call. "Stop," she touches my wrist as I flip. "That one's good too."

We narrow seventy-two prints down to five by the time Jay finishes his second hamburger. Then I haul out the bests from the other seventeen rolls.

I study the pictures really closely. Choosing the wrong one will mean no audition with *Ms Mode*, no cover shot, maybe no career. I picture myself dressed like my mother, working day after day in a dull grey office. "Jay, go and get me a magnifying glass from Mr. Miyata's science lab."

"Sure, Kim."

I eat my salad as we wait.

"They're all perfect," Julie says. "It's just a matter of which pose and mood captures you best."

I frown. Jay comes back with the magnifying glass and we all pore over the pictures again.

Finally we vote on the shot. It's the one where my mouth turns slightly at the corner, the one that makes me seem just a little smug.

"Look, Mr. Miyata's over there. You can return the magnifying glass to him now," I hand it back to Jay.

Jay shrugs his shoulders and pockets it. "Don't think so. He doesn't know I have it."

I shake my head at him and let him pick one of the big-eared boxer short pictures for his locker.

"Did you remember the permission note?" Julie asks.

My face turns hot. "Permission note. You think she'll really ask for one?"

"Don't be a baby," Julie answers. "I can help with the wording, but I'm not writing or signing it."

I've been carrying a sheet of Mom's stationery in my bag all day for this purpose. I take it out and stare at it. No guts.

"Do you know Rebecca did a fashion show at the mall a couple of weeks ago? She modelled an evening gown and got to keep it," Julie tells me.

I'm picturing myself walking across a runway in a gown, and somehow I get a flash of my nightmare — the petunias, Mom's office, that filing cabinet . . . I just *have* to do this. I pick up the pen.

"Hey, I can do that," Jay says. "Give it here. You have to write with big loops. That shows confidence . . . "

"Dear Ms Chev . . . " Julie dictates and Jay loops.

It'll be all right. My parents will understand once I earn big money as a model. I mean, that's what Dad wants me to get good grades for, after all. To get into a university and then from there to get a good job.

"There. All set," Julie says after Jay signs in huge sloppy letters.

"Yes. Only we should get there well before her closing time — say five-thirty. Which is going to make it awful tight for me." I sigh. "And wouldn't you know it, we have double gym last two periods today."

"That's right, I forgot! Are you going to have time to shower and get ready and all that?"

I chew at the nail on my pointer finger. *Two hours to get ready is nothing for a model.* Leaving out travel time, I had about forty-five minutes. "There's just no way I can look my best in that short a time." I frown hard. "I'm just going to have to figure something else out."

"We're starting cross country today, girls," Ms Bryant tells us later that afternoon.

"Oh, just shoot me," I whisper to Julie.

She shakes her head in sympathy.

"So I want you to run down Mountaingrove, around Fisher, back by Augustine, across Upper Middle and then back through the shortcut to school."

"I'd like to see her do it first," Julie mutters under her breath.

"Wouldn't be a pretty sight." I shudder and shake my head. Ms Bryant ripples with muscles. She can probably run it twice.

"Line up, girls." The class straggles into forma-
tion. Kids moan and groan. "Remember, you can go
at your own pace. I'll meet you at the checkpoint on
Augustine. Ready? Off you go."

Some of the browners shoot off right away.

"Hey, get a load of Andrea in shorts. She looks
almost human now that she's lost weight," Julie
says.

But I have lots more than Andrea to think about.
Checkpoint at Augustine, hmm. I can just leave my
backpack and clothes behind for one night and . . .

"Hurry up. Get moving. C'mon, let's not hang
back," Ms Bryant calls. I notice her chuck Andrea
on the shoulder as she trundles by. "You're looking
fit today."

Now I have to look at Andrea. So she's actually
showing a waistline, big deal.

"She must have lost a ton of weight," Julie says.

We jog out the door together. A bunch of the guys
see us heading out. They whistle and jeer. I hate
being on display like that when I'm running in
cheap school gym clothes that do absolutely nothing for my figure.

Jay winks at me and then notices Andrea for the
second time. He just stares. I make a face at him as
I race by.

"Let's go, Julie," I say as we gain on Andrea. And
then I can't resist and it just pops out. "Moooo!" I
call as we pass her by. I don't even look back.

"You're so mean," Julie tells me as we keep running. But she says it with a smile in her voice.

"Oh, I'm just encouraging her in my own little way." I run harder and gain on Julie too.

"What's your rush?" she asks as she huffs to keep up.

"I'm heading for the checkpoint. Then I'm splitting. I need the extra time to get ready. Cover for me in case."

I've never run so hard around those blocks. "Pace yourself!" Ms Bryant calls to me as she presses her stopwatch.

Pace myself nothing. The moment I pass her I duck through the shortcut through the woods and run the rest of the way home.

My knees feel like jelly when I finally step into the shower. I'll have to skip the conditioner, I think, mentally speeding up my beauty routine. I shampoo and rinse quickly, then grab my blue mini. My pantyhose stick to my legs because I don't dry off well enough, and as I tug them up I put a thumbnail through. Or what's left of a thumbnail. I've bitten that one down pretty far. Still, a ladder races up the leg.

Sigh! I riffle through my drawers for another pair. Finally I pull on some without any damage. Four o'clock.

Usually I air dry my hair just a bit, but today there's no time. I hang my head upside down and aim the hot air at the base of my hair. "Blow drying hair upside down will add fullness." Tip 28 from 50 Ways to Improve on Nature.

I put on my make-up faster than I've ever done before. Oops. I dab a bit of mascara on my cheek. I wipe at it and smear the black spot more. I dab a cotton swab in some cold cream and wipe at it, but that makes a hole in my foundation.

I can't take my base off and start all over, so I patch the hole, adding some more foundation. I frown into my make-up mirror. *Is this how it started with my mother? Too much time and trouble to look good? The quick make-up job? Next I'll be buying pre-matched clothing.* Too bad, it'll have to do. I bite at my baby fingernail, but it doesn't satisfy. There's nothing left to chew.

Great, great, great. Time to go. I hate running and getting all breathless and sweaty, but I really have to zoom. I barely make it in time for the bus. The bus turns out to be the slowest one in the world. I stare at my watch each time we stop for a light or at another stop. Finally, finally the bus rolls up to the building that matches the address.

Suite 360, that means third floor, but I can't see an elevator anywhere. Up and up the stone stairs, I try to stay graceful. This feels like a bad dream. CHEVRON AGENCY, the black letters on the door read. I knock, then press the buzzer, then wait.

The door opens and a women dressed in a

cherry-coloured silk suit smiles at me. "Hello, I'm Elaine Chev and you are?"

"Kimberly Rainer. I'm here for the open call."

"Yes, yes, come in." She motions with her hand to a chair and I notice her fingernails immediately. They're perfect, well-shaped, a centimetre longer than her fingers, and they're manicured French style, the tips painted a white shade, the base a natural gloss.

"You brought pictures and a note from your parents?" she asks.

I nod and hand her the forged letter and an envelope of four photos. The fifth one is now in the mail with my fifty words about why I want to be a *Ms Mode* cover girl.

The telephone rings then and Ms Chev picks up, still holding my photos between her French tips. "Lianne? Good to hear from you. It went well, did it?" She frowns as she taps my photos. "Your last cheque? Let me just look at my file. Yes . . . here we are . . . It went in the mail this morning. You should get it Monday, latest."

Can it be? Is it possible? Lianne Ulan, my fave supermodel, on the other end? I want to hug myself with joy to think that I am at the agency that's on the other side of that phone call.

"Don't be a stranger," Ms Chev says. *"Ciao!"* Then she hangs up.

I watch her expression as she quickly flips

through the pictures. "Well, you'll simply have to have professional shots taken. These can go on file for now, but I'd like to replace them as quickly as possible."

So much for Julie's photography skills and seventeen rolls of film. Only what do I look like right now? I wish I could check in a mirror somewhere. Everything about me feels hurried and hot. I must look awful.

"Let's find out a little about you, shall we? What's your favourite subject in school?" she asks me. "How are your grades? Do you have any outside interests? Sports? Do you take dance?"

None, low, no, none, no. I know I sound too boring. But she nods and fills in blanks as I answer. The interview does not go the way I want it to. Still Ms Chev smiles at me. I need to fill out my address, phone, weight, height, sizes — shoes, waist, bust, hips, dress and even glove. Then she checks over my information.

"So I think we should make the appointment with our photographer right away. I need a cheque for two hundred dollars."

"Two hundred dollars?"

"Yes, and you read the part about how we work? Your fee goes to us, we take our twenty percent and send you your share within thirty days."

"I don't have two hundred dollars."

"Kimberly, you'll likely earn that back with your

first assignment. If we set up the photo session now, by the time you have to pay, you may have earned the money already. Shall I make the appointment?" She picks up the telephone receiver.

"I'm accepted then?" I ask.

She smiles. "Of course. You're beautiful."

All my rushed hotness melts away then. I feel relief and then such a high as everything inside me flies up in excitement, like a roller coaster climbing up. *I am beautiful. I can model. If there's nothing else in this world for me, I have that!*

"Um, I'll just have to see about the money first. I . . . My mother didn't realize there would be a fee, so I just need to check."

She shrugs her shoulders and eyebrows at the same time. "Well, just get back to me when you have the money." She looks down on my application and writes something on the form. Then she stops again and looks up. "Oh and one thing, Kimberly."

"Yes, Ms Chev?"

"You will stop biting your nails."

chapter 8

"Mom, please. It's only two hundred dollars and it means my whole future to me." I stick my baby fingernail in my mouth, but the taste of the Bite-stop shoots through to my nostrils. The flavour is awful — mouse pee and medicine. I spit into a piece of tissue.

"It is not your 'whole future,' Kim, trust me." Mom glances from the steering wheel to me. "You haven't even begun to explore your talents. Looks just are not everything."

Not to her, obviously. I lift an eyebrow at her as I sigh.

Her eyes look sorry — pitying, maybe — but that doesn't help. "And we have to discuss it with your father."

"You know what he'll say. I should concentrate on school." I stick my index finger in my mouth. "Ack, phooey."

"Honey, you're just too young to be working, anyway. I mean, baby-sitting, fine, but real work — "

"You don't understand, Mom. I hate looking after little kids. Fashion is my life!" I lift my thumb to my mouth but stop in the nick of time.

The car rolls into the school parking lot.

She turns to me again. "No, it's *you* who don't understand. You have no idea what kind of life modelling is."

I stop and turn to stare her straight in the eye. "Oh, and *you* do?"

"Yes, as a matter of fact, I do. Listen, right now I'm running late, but we'll talk more tonight. Okay?" Her eyes look pleading, but I can see her mouth looks set.

"Oh, what's the point? You're never going to change your mind anyway." I shake my head at her and toss my hair back as I dash away from the car.

"What's the matter, Kimmm?" Jay asks as he cranes his neck around to eyeball Lauren walking by with stick-woman Stephanie.

I slap my binder on his head. "You're the matter. You drool over anything in skirts."

"Hey, that's not true."

"I stand corrected." I give Lauren a cold stare, taking in her farmer outfit. "Anything in overalls. Anything at all," I add when I see him checking out Andrea again. Her dieting is working. I can see the vague shape of a cheekbone in her puffy apple cheeks. For some reason that just makes me madder. "You don't care a bit about me."

"I'd die for you. You know that." His eyes believe what he says as he looks into mine. Only his lips smile a little.

And then I can't help smiling back. "Would you have two hundred dollars you could lend me?"

"Two hundred! No. Sorry — Mom found my bankbook in my jeans pocket when she did the laundry." He shrugs his shoulders. "I had to return the money I withdrew and I'm paying the rest back with allowance."

"You were my last hope. Julie doesn't have any money either. I won't be able to have the professional shots taken."

"Wait a minute, Kim. Back up. That agency's *taking* you? All you need is a lousy two hundred bucks and you'll be a model?"

I nod glumly.

"You must have some bank account somewhere too. You know, where your mom and dad stashed your birthday money back when you were a baby?"

"Yes, and the money Grandma Rainer left me in her will. But it's not really for everyday things. It's for my future."

"Well, that's what you'll be using it for, isn't it?"

Hmm. Jay has a point, actually. It *is* for my future — the future I plan for me, anyway. And if Mom and Dad don't plan the same one — well, that's *their* problem, not mine.

The bell rings then. I rush to class, kids jostling me in the halls, with no time even to think much more about it. Especially when the first class is math. That's bad enough, but today Ms Smyrnious is handing out the tests. I write down my name and then the date in the right-hand corner, underlining it with my ruler. In the centre, I write Math Test and underline that twice. Back in Grade 5 the teacher insisted we do our work that way and I thought Ms Smyrnious might appreciate it too. For each problem I write the number inside the margin, with a bracket around it. I indent the first line.

Ned rides on a donkey, I repeat to myself as I try to divide the fractions. *Ned stands for the numerator and the donkey for the denominator.* Dad taught me that. So fine, now I know the names of the fractions. How am I supposed to divide them, again?

I take a peek over Stephanie's shoulders. Her writing is just so hard to read. As I strain to read it, I can feel the backs of my eyes getting sore. Is that a 7 over the 8 or a 4? I guess a 4.

Little hammers pound behind my eyes now, and my head starts to ache. Ms Smyrnious looks at me strangely as I squint against the bright light. My stomach turns. I can't stick around. I know I'm going to hurl. And my hair hasn't even crackled its usual "headache coming" warning. I raise my hand weakly.

"Yes, Kimberly."

"Can I go lie down in the nurse's office?"

She frowns. "If you have to. You know you'll have to make up the test some time."

I stand up on shaking legs, trying to remember to

be graceful. But I really have to hurry. I walk my long-legged stride as quickly as I can without running. In the nurse's office I barely make it to the toilet to throw up. Then I lie down on the hard little bed with the grey scratchy blanket and fall asleep.

Mom says later when she finds me in my room sleeping, "Why didn't you call me? I would have left work early and picked you up."

"That's okay. I slept at school. Then Julie's mom drove me home."

"What did you eat last night and this morning? You know what they said at the headache clinic — you have to log what you eat so they can see if it's certain foods that trigger it."

"Mom, I'm going back to sleep now or I'll be sick again. Okay?" I don't even register what she answers. For all I know it's math, not food, that brings on the headaches. Right now I just feel exhausted and want to fall into that big black hole that always happens when I have a headache.

Mom feels so bad for me that she goes out and buys me a stack of fashion magazines. I find them next morning with a smiley-face note on my night table. She even bought that adult one, *Metropolitan*, the one where the models have the cleavage of Andrea with the skin-and-bones body of Stephanie. Not that many people are really built like that — I read somewhere that the models use surgical tape to get that effect. Yuck.

The model on this cover wears a leopard skin dress that clings to her body as though *she's* the leopard. The slit down the front drops all the way to her navel. Such a cheap look. Huh! I flip through to look at the ads. A strong sweet smell cracks through my beigeness, threatening to get my headache pounding again. I rip out the page with the cologne strip and throw it in the trash.

How to Tell if Your Mate Is Cheating is this month's quiz in *Metro*. I toss it aside and pick up *Seventeen*, sniffing for cologne strips. Good, none.

The ads in this magazine use really hot guys. They all look older than Jay but their eyes smile just like his. He should be a model like me, I think. Then I remember. Two hundred dollars. How am I going to do it?

Seventeen's quiz is Are Your 'Rents Driving You Crazy? Well, duh. That's a no-brainer.

Still, I sit up in bed and grab a ballpoint from my desk.

You're out late for a rock concert and you miss your last bus. Do your parents:

(a) come and get you, no questions asked?

(b) rant and rave and tell you to take a cab? The fare will be coming out of your allowance for the next year.

(c) not even answer the phone? They go to sleep at 10 o'clock.

Okay, so they get (a) on that one. They'd probably both get up, grab a coffee at the doughnut shop and head over.

You ask your parents for lunch money, they:

(a) hand you five dollars and ask for change at the end of the day.
(b) suggest you make a peanut butter sandwich.
(c) don't have change for a $20 so they give it to you and never ask for anything back.

Well, of course, Mom always hands me tens and twenties, because she never carries change or makes lunches and she and I both feel the same about peanut butter. It's just too high in fat.

You need to work on a project with your opposite-sex partner. Your parents:

(a) insist you leave your bedroom door open.
(b) ask that you not work at the house when they're not there.
(c) trust you entirely.

My parents are (c). But why not? I don't give them any reason not to trust me and, really, the other options are too much work. They're too busy to always be checking on me.

You want to go to a slumber party at a friend's. Your parents:

(a) need to have a parent-to-parent interview.
(b) donate a couple of bags of chips and tell you to have a good time.

(c) call twice during the night to check up on you.

I don't really do a lot of sleepovers, never mind sleeping over at places where I don't know the people that well. Bringing chips — hmm, no, that's not something my mother would suggest either. I brought a dozen fresh bagels to Julie's last birthday sleepover. Answer (b) is still the closest to how my parents would react. They're really doing great on this quiz till I get to the last part.

Over dinner, you tell them about something really exciting that's going on in your life and they:

(a) tell you to pass the butter.
(b) lean forward and get as excited as you are.
(c) cross-examine you and tell you why you shouldn't be excited at all.

They fit (c) exactly. The only thing my parents care about is school and my future as they see it. There should be a question about how often your parents lecture you about grades. They'd lose a lot of points on that one.

You dress up special for a killer date. Your 'rents:

(a) grab a camera and/or camcorder to record the event.
(b) suggest to you that your dress might be a little too tight and/or short and that you really shouldn't wear so much make-up.
(c) tell you that you look "nice" while barely peering over their newspapers.

Maybe for a prom Dad might put his newspaper down and bring out his digital camera, but for the most part, he'd be a (c).

It's your birthday and there's a designer watch you really want. When you ask for it, your 'rents:

(a) say it's too expensive but give you a sizeable money donation towards it. Maybe with relatives' money prezzies, and a year of baby-sitting, you'll be able buy it yourself.

(b) give you a cheap imitation they picked up at a flea market, telling you no one can tell the difference, plus it was half the price and waterproof.

(c) buy something entirely different. They either don't know or don't care what you want — or worse, totally disapprove.

It's the last question that really gets to me. I mean, I really loved getting the glamour shot taken last year. Having my hair styled and my face done, dressing up in different looks, posing and then see-ing the results on the computer monitor — it was all great and a *total* surprise, for which I credit my mother. Sometimes she seems to really know what I want. At least she tries — although my father usually gets to her first.

Just look what happened when I asked for a *Ms Mode* subscription. I know it wouldn't have cost as much as the book my father bought me, *The Ten Habits of the Highly Effective Teenager.* But Dad said the magazine was stupid and he didn't want my head filled with the garbage they printed in it.

He thinks everything I want or do is stupid. And my mother wants to "talk over" the two hundred dollars for the professional shots? Hmph. If Dad has any say in it, I already know the answer.

I add up their score now. Oh yeah, they score forty-two points, which puts them in the middle category: Concerned but Clueless:

> Have patience with your 'rents. You've grown up a lot over the last few years and they may be having just a little trouble catching up. Keep the communication lines open and eventually they'll come around.

Oh, sure. They'll come around when it's too late for me to do anything. I'll be lying in that grey morgue drawer by the time they come around.

My Dad comes home at lunch time with takeout chicken noodle for me from the Soup Nutsie near his office. I decide to "open the lines of communication" with him then. "Mmm, this soup is so good, Daddy," I say in between spoonfuls.

"Only the best," he agrees as he eats too. "You're feeling better?"

"Much." So far so good. "Actually, Daddy I was thinking . . . I'd like to try a part-time modelling job. You know, earn a little extra money." My father starts choking on his chicken noodle, but I keep

going. "Do you think I could have two hundred dollars for some portfolio shots?"

"What? Kimberly, no!" His eyes are watering as
he sputters. "You've been talking to your mother,
haven't you? What did she tell you?"

"Nothing, only that we'd discuss it with you."

Dad chug-a-lugs some water as he continues to
shake his head. "No way, no how, no daughter of
mine!"

The lines of communication go zap. In my mind
I see my body neatly tucked away in that filing
cabinet. I'll just die if I never even try.

That's when I finally decide. When Dad leaves
for work again I head for the den and the desk
where my parents write out all the cheques.

Drawer number one, slam! Drawer number two,
slam! Drawer number three. Ahh! There it is. A pink
bankbook with a white bunny on the cover. A line
from the quiz comes back to me:

> You've grown up a lot over the last few years
> and they may be having just a little trouble
> catching up.

What an understatement! I mean, a bunny-rabbit
bankbook! I open it up to the last page and frown.
Last deposit is at Christmas. My other grandmother gave me some money. There's over forty-
eight hundred dollars there now. Wow! I can easily
take two hundred out — they'll never notice. At

77

least, not till next birthday or Christmas. I check my watch. Three more hours till they come home again — there's plenty of time. I'll hurry to the bank before I change my mind.

chapter 9

Too bad Jay wasn't around when I tried to reach him. I mean, he's the expert on handling bank tellers. He just smiles and looks adorable for them. I chew on my thumbnail for a moment and hardly taste the bitterness as I try to think like Jay. Wear the blue dress, blue looks sincere. But it's not hanging in my closet. I wore it the other day. Maybe in the dryer? I slip through the kitchen into the laundry room and tug at a wire that someone has rigged as a dryer handle. Hard to believe that with all the nothing my parents fill their lives with, they still haven't gotten their act together on this one simple thing. I grab the dress and head back to my room to change. Over my head the dress goes as I check the full-length mirror. No wrinkles — good, good, I decide, slipping on some high-heeled shoes.

Then I sit down at my vanity and flip on the light switch underneath the mirror. The light bulbs burst into tiny stars surrounding my face. Make-up to look older, but not too much, I tell myself. I try to recall the advice I read in *Teen* just a couple of issues ago: The Girl Next Door — How to Get that Fresh-Scrubbed Look. A quick brush of blush across my cheekbones. Not too much — don't want to look like I feel guilty. Then I curl my lashes and layer on a thick coat of mascara. No eyeliner or shadow, I decide. It might look too harsh in the fluorescent light of the bank. Sugarberry lip gloss — that was definitely recommended in the article — I roll some on my lips and then blot it slightly on a tissue.

I look perfect. No one will suspect I'm withdrawing college funds without my parent's permission. I take a deep breath and check my watch. By now school's out, so I make a phone call. "Hello, Julie? Feel like joining me for a triple-fruit frozen yogurt? My treat," I add, remembering how generous Jay was to me on the day he went to the bank.

I have no trouble convincing her. We hop a bus together, my pink-and-white bunny bankbook tucked safely in my bag.

"You know what you should do," Julie says as we step into the branch where my parents do their banking.

I quickly scan the room to make sure neither got off early. The coast is clear. "What, what?" I ask Julie impatiently as I step into line.

"You should get one of those cards so that you can use the machine or even pay stores directly."

I shake my head. "No, no. I just need the two hundred dollars. I'm not making a career of this." Suddenly a teller opens and calls to me.

I hand her the bunny book and ask for the

money. She frowns at me for a moment and I feel my shoulders knot. I can't shift my eyes away from her or she'll know something's up.

"You didn't fill out a withdrawal slip," the teller grumbles.

"Oh, oh, I'm sorry. I forgot." My hand over my mouth, my face flushing, I'm sure I'm the picture of embarrassment.

And it works. She scribbles out the information on a slip and passes it over to me. "Sign please."

I smile and feel bubbles form inside me, fill up and float so high. Bright pink bubbles. There's not a trace of grey as she counts out the money and slips it to me.

Then suddenly they all pop as I spot him over near the bank machine His head is ducked and some woman I don't know stands beside him. He's keying something into the automatic teller machine. I'd know that curly grey hair anywhere.

He's a chubby, round-faced man with a poorly fitting brown suit. But he's got a booming principal's voice that carries everywhere. I've heard him yell at Jay, and his voice just about fills the house. He really scares me. What will he think if he sees me here?

Julie walks over. "Guess who's over there!" she tells me.

"Keep your voice down," I whisper. "I already saw him. I don't want him to see me here.

Especially since he caught Jay taking money from his college account. He'll guess right away why I'm here."

"Anything else I can do for you?" the teller asks me. She's tapping a pen, waiting for me to clear from her wicket.

"Um, no, no." I step away, careful to keep my face away from the bank machines.

"Turn around quickly," Julie whispers. "Looks to me like Jay's dad can't afford to make any trouble for you!"

I flash a quick look towards Mr. Friessen and see now what Julie is talking about. The lady next to him moves even closer to him, too close if you ask me.

"And he grounded Jay for a month for breaking into a chat room. Who does he think he is?" Julie says.

"Shh, come on! Let's just get out of here." I practically have to pull Julie out of the mall and drag her to the bus stop.

"Hey, hey! What about my frozen yogurt?" she asks.

"After we deliver the money to the agency. I want to get this over with."

Chevron is not in the best part of town, and just like me, Julie's not impressed as we climb the three flights of stairs to the office of Elaine Chev.

"I'm telling you, she was talking to Lianne Ulan on the other line. Her office may not look great, but she's dealing with some high-class models here."

"And Rebecca's certainly doing all right by them," Julie agrees as we push through the door.

"Yes? Can I help you? Do you have an appointment?" Elaine asks us. Today she's wearing a royal blue suit and little golden half-glasses attached to a chain. She peers over them to look at me. But it doesn't seem like she recognizes me at all.

"I . . . um . . . brought the money," I tell her.

"Money?" she asks.

"Yes, for the photo shoot." I take out the roll of bills and put them on the desk.

"Cash?" she asks as she stares at the bills.

It's the wrong thing to do. I can tell by the way she says it. "Sorry, my mother ran out of cheques this morning and she was running late . . . "

"You are?" She's still peering.

"Kimberly Rainer."

She takes in the fingers holding the bills now. "Ah, yes, the nail biter. I'll write you out a receipt. Let's get you an appointment with Gunther, shall we?" She picks up the phone and punches in some numbers as she removes a receipt book from her desk. She writes as she listens. "Yes, Gunther darling. I have a breathtaking beauty here. Yes. Great hair and a wonderful mouth. Mmm." She covers the mouthpiece and addresses me. "You want an after-school appointment, don't you. What time is good?"

Before Mom and Dad get home, I think. "Four-thirty?"

She repeats the time into the phone. "You're booked up solid for the next two weeks! I understand, yes with Mother's Day and all. Of course. When? Monday, May twelfth. Wonderful, Gunther. Thank you so much. *Ciao!*" She takes another piece of paper from a little yellow pad and scribbles down the address, handing it to me. "Bring three changes of clothing with accessories, an exercise or bodysuit, something glamorous and something young and girl-next-door. Gunther may also create different looks for you with outfits he has lying around. And here's your receipt." The phone rings again before she can dismiss us.

Julie and I look at each other, wondering whether we should slip away, but then Ms Chev holds up a finger, signalling us to wait. "I have the perfect model for you standing right in front of me. She's young and fresh and a perfect size five."

"Sometimes I take three," I say softly.

She shakes her head furiously and holds that same finger to her lips to shush me. Then she talks to the person on the other end again. "I can fax some snapshots to you. They're not professional though. Uh huh . . . Uh huh." Now she brightens. "Friday, May ninth. Eleven o'clock? Perfect." She cradles the receiver and looks up at me. "Well, you're in luck, aren't you? You'll earn your money back before the actual photo shoot."

"Um, Friday's a school day," I mumble. Julie elbows me hard. "Um, yes, eleven is great."

I feel the bright pink bubbles inside me again. I'm really going to be a model! It's what I've dreamt about for so long, taking the first steps down that runway, away from my parents' boring world. Skipping school's not a big deal when it has to do with your future. I can fake a headache. This is exactly what I save them for. And it's all so easy.

"You'll need to take a cab to this address, there are no bus connections," Ms Chev hands me another yellow slip of paper. "It's Valentino and Durkin's. Get there at least fifteen minutes early."

"Wow, yes, Ms Chev. Thank you, Ms Chev." Then another thing strikes me. I have no cash left for the cab. "Can I have my money back then?" I ask.

"Sorry no. I do have to process the paperwork for income tax purposes. You'll have your fee back in no time, don't worry."

"Um, sure. Okay, bye."

Julie and I head down the stairs again. "Can you lend me some cash?" I ask her as we head back for the bus stop.

"Hey, what about you treating me to yogurt?" Julie raises an eyebrow at me, but smiles.

"Hey, don't sweat it. I want to celebrate all this, and I'll definitely pay you back. It's just for the cab ride. I can't very well ask my parents, can I?"

"Sorry, Kim. I don't have nearly enough for cab fare on me." The bus rolls up and we get on.

We drive by a large billboard that asks, "Worried about your future?" Underneath the lettering a pleasant looking suit type smiles over a desk at a woman with frown wrinkles. "Talk to your representative at the City Savings and Loan," the caption reads.

The bus *sishes* to a stop at the mall where we got on. The solution to my money problems becomes clear to me. I'm on my way up after all — these cash shortages are all just temporary.

chapter 10

"Have you seen a doctor about your headaches?"
Ms Smyrnious asks me the Friday of my first
modelling job. I don't blame her for being suspicious. This headache comes only a couple of weeks
after the real one. Too close. That's why I usually
tough them out. Ms Smyrnious looks at me like the
lady on the City Savings and Loan billboard, forehead all wrinkled, eyes squinting.

I'm not expecting the third degree from her. "I . . .
I'm supposed to keep a journal. To keep track of
what I eat or what I'm doing that might be trigger-
ing them. But the doctor hasn't really found anything specific. She thinks they're just caused by
tension."

"All right, you can go to the office. You still owe
me that math quiz, though, Kimberly."

So she thinks math is inspiring my headaches.
Could be . . . At least she has no real clue as to why
I need to cut today's class. The secretary frowns,
too, when she hears that I have to leave. "My
mom's coming to pick me up. I've already called
her."

She nods and I head out the side door near the

opposite parking lot so she can't watch as I hop a bus to my parents' bank again.

This time there's no one I know at the machines or in line, but I duck my head all the same. I also fill out the withdrawal slip, so the teller won't crab. *One hundred dollars* I write, in large loopy hand-writing the way Jay told me to the last time. Who really knows what cab fare will amount to, after all? I don't feel safe this time till the cab rolls up and I slip into the back seat. Then I feel the pink bubbles rising inside me.

I'm a model going to a shoot! I cross my legs and smile at the driver. "Valentino and Durkin's," I tell him, hoping he'll recognize the name of some famous photography studio where he drives models like Lianne Ulan all the time. But he hesitates and waits for the street address.

I give it to him and we roll. Past the stores, past the office buildings. My dad's office even. I slink down in the seat. Into the industrial area, past some warehouses, right to the end of a street.

"You're sure you want this address, Miss?" the driver ask as we pull into the lot.

I check the number on the yellow slip of paper, then the number on the bricks. I also spot a paper sign in the window. "Valentino and Durkin's Textiles."

"Yes, thank you, this is it."

He turns around in the seat. "You sure you don't

want me to wait while you check?"

"No, that will be fine." I hand him a couple of bills that include a generous tip. Jay Friessen's not the only one with class.

Then I slide out of the car and walk towards the door with hips pushed forward and long strides, in case the photographer is watching. I try to pull the door open gracefully, only it won't budge. I press a buzzer to the side. No answer. I press again. Finally the door opens.

A nerdy type opens the door. He wears thick horn-rimmed glasses and his brown eyes swim behind them. His black hair hangs in long half curls around his ears and he grins at me with large white teeth. His upper lip rides as high as Lauren's. Ugh! He reaches out his hand towards me as if he wants to touch me. I shrink back.

"I'm Pete Valentino. The owner. You the model?"

I nod and the words float out of my mouth as though riding on those pink bubbles. "Yes, I am the model." Somehow I'm expecting a deafening round of applause, flashes from cameras and people calling, "Hurrah, look how beautiful! Of course, she's the model."

Instead I get, "C'mon back to the showroom. I'll show you the threads."

We walk down a narrow grey hallway, which almost reminds me of the one in my bad dream. Then we cross over a kind of bridge walkway.

Below us there are rows and rows of black sewing machines rat-a-tatting to the touch of some hunch-backed women. Their expressions are all serious, as though the troubles of the world are being hammered out by the needles they control with their foot pedals. Their jobs look even worse than my parents'.

"Hurry up, some buyers are already waiting in my office," Nerdman tells me.

We push through a door and there are two racks of clothing there. He squints at me and nudges me towards one of the racks.

"This one first," he points to a polyester Bermuda short set in emerald green, complete with a matching vest and a contrasting yellow T-shirt. It's something my grandmother would wear to play golf. "Then this one," he points to a fake suede culottes set. "This one." A jungle print dress of some kind. "And the button-down jumpsuit. And then nightwear." He pulls out a leopard print peignoir that reminds me of that cover on the *Metropolitan* magazine my mother bought me.

"Um, where's the changing room?" I ask.

"Are you kidding? There's no time for all that." He frowns. "Oh — that's right. You're the new girl, aren't you?"

I shrug my shoulders. "I've done runway before." I don't tell him it was for the school fashion show.

"Well," he shakes a finger at me, "no underwear

— it makes lines. You're pretty pale, too." He reaches around to the drawer of a large steel desk and pulls out some wrinkled dark pantyhose. "Here, wear these."

The door bursts open now and a short broad man saunters in with a thin dark-skinned girl. There's a loud smell of spicy aftershave surrounding him, so I try not to breathe in when he walks close. I don't want it kicking off a headache. He points the girl towards the other rack of clothing, then turns towards me, but doesn't really look at me. "Girls, hurry up."

Then he grabs Nerdman by the arm and pulls him out the door.

The thin girl immediately strips to a thong and then even it comes off. My mouth drops open. By the time I close it again she's dressed in a canary-coloured pantsuit. "Better drop your drawers, honey. I'm not looking, but they sure will be if you're not out there on the double."

I step behind the rack and put a thumb through the pantyhose as I pull them up. Luckily the shorts cover the run, at least for now. Horrible fabrics. Awful colours.

"I'm Nina. You are . . . ?" the girl asks as she extends her hand.

"Kimberly." I shake her hand.

"Could you fit me?" She turns and hands me some straight pins. "I'm a size three. This seems like at least a five. Do it along the seam so it doesn't ruin the . . . *hem* line." She winks at me and I tuck in some material at the back. It's hard to do while she's wearing the top. "Just a sec, I have an idea." I whip out some hair clips I have in my bag. They're bright-coloured butterflies and they hide the gather in the back perfectly. "Perfect!" I tell her. "See."

"No time now, Kimberly. Let's rock and roll."

She leads the way into another room where there are five men and two women standing, clipboards in hand, sipping from Styrofoam cups.

"Ladies and gentlemen, from our Ultra Sport line, cruise wear." Nerdman waves his hand towards us.

Ultra Sport . . . That's a brand sold at Bargain Bart outlets. Why would anyone shop there for cruise wear?

Just then one woman grabs the end of my vest and rubs her thumb and pointer finger across the fabric.

"Washable, crease resistant," Nerdman comments.

She scribbles something down on her clipboard.

"Turn around, girls," the broad older man says without looking at us. "The shorts come in cranberry, toasted almond and butter. The pantsuit in indigo, mint and cherry."

"I like the butterfly snaps. Do they come in other

colours?" one buyer asks. The other buyers seem interested too.

"What butterflies?" The older guy grabs Nina. "Why did you put those insects on my line?"

I wince. "I'm sorry, I did that. The line of the fabric wasn't right, so I — "

"Enough. I don't pay you to design!" he huffs at me.

Now the buyer cuts in, chuckling. "Maybe you should, Herb. She seems pretty good to me."

Herb rolls his eyes and shakes his head. "Models with brains, who needs 'em."

But I'm not a brainer, honest, I want to tell him. Only as we continue walking around and around, I also think, hey I *am* good at design. Ms Ferris said something about that in family studies too.

Nerdman motions to us if we stop moving. After about five minutes the older man calls, "Next outfits, ladies." He snaps his fingers to hurry us along.

The next two outfits, Nina "fits" me, only with straight pins, no clips.

"This is the worst clothing I've ever worn," I tell her. "It doesn't fit right, the fabric is terrible, the colours are bad — "

"Shhh!" she says just as the door bangs open.

"Chop, chop, ladies. Come on!" It's the old guy and he stands there until we follow him. I'm reaching back to zip up the jungle dress as I'm walking. The old man helps me with fumbling cigar-shaped fingers as we're about to step through the door into the "showroom." By this time everyone is eating smoked meat sandwiches, and the smell of pickles and mustard wafts around us.

One man waves his sandwich at me as he talks, his mouth slightly open. "That print come in any other shades?"

"Rainforest, kahlua and mandarin," Nerdman answers, handing him a batch of fabric swatches. Such high-class colours for such low-budget fashion. I force myself not to shake my head.

The crowning experience has to be parading around in the leopard-print peignoir. The neckline plunges and the fabric is skimpy. I fold my arms across my chest as I walk through into the office.

Nerdman grabs both my hands and pulls them away, swinging me around as though I'm dancing with him.

Nina's wearing a shortie baby doll in a peach tone, but her arms rest by her side. If she weren't prancing around in almost-see-through sleepwear, I think I would die a few more deaths.

It's only a job to them, I tell myself as I face the glazed stares of the men and women. I swirl between the desks, the cheap nylon billowing out from me. It's almost over, I think, and hey — I'm a professional now. I can smile yet one more time for these people.

"Nice, girls." Cigar fingers snap at us and gesture to the door. I head out with a sigh of relief. It's over now. No job can ever be as bad. I mean, I never wanted to do showroom modelling anyway, but in such a grubby sweatshop — ugh! At least I earned the photo money back. And the next assignment's got to be better. Maybe I can insist on runway or print work only. Yeah, that's what I'll do.

But as we step into the back room, Nerdman rolls in another rack from the other door. It's covered with a dull grey sheet. "You're not through yet, girls. This represents our top-secret new line. You're the first of the public to see." He pulls the sheet away. "And the first to have the privilege of wearing our new Wild Reflections."

Wild Reflections, I think, as he hands me a purple jogging suit. The name of the line sounds like . . . and that's when I notice the tiny pastel flowers embroidered on the sleeve. I gasp. I can't believe I'm actually going to model a low-end knockoff of my mother's favourite clothing line.

I force a smile onto my face and reach for the hanger.

chapter 11

"So how did it go?" Julie asks me on Monday. Her family always goes away Mother's Day weekend, so it's the first time we have to discuss it. Her eyes shine with admiration. Her mouth is slightly open, almost as though she's panting to hear about my success. Her reaction is so much what I'd hoped for from the rest of the world, I can't disappoint her with the truth.

"Fine, fine. Well . . . I mean . . . it was showroom work. Not what I want to do at all. I really want to do runway and print modelling." Applause roaring from the crowds as I strut across a lit-up runway, cameras flashing, glossy photographs of me staring back from teen fashion magazines — it's what I imagine will still happen to me. After all, Elaine Chev represents Jan Johannsen and Lianne Ulan. I'm sure they don't model for places like Valentino and Durkin's rag shop. Working at the Halton Board Office would have just as much glamour. I smile at Julie. "Anyway, I'll have something to put on my résumé when I meet the people from *Ms Mode.*"

"You're so lucky, Kimberly!"

I smile at her much the same way as I did yesterday at all those buyers. Someday . . . someday . . . I think about page 35 in *Ms Mode* and cross my fingers. Magazine modelling has to be different, doesn't it? And maybe professional photos will get me better jobs. "Tonight's my session with Gunther," I remind her.

"Oh wow, right! You'll have to tell me all about that. Pay attention to the cameras and lenses he uses, okay? I can't wait!"

"Me either." I check the school clock. "And only seven more hours!" I sigh as I head into the classroom.

Ms Smyrnious approaches me first the moment I sit down at my desk. "How about making up that math quiz after school today?" she asks.

"Oh my gosh. I'd love to but I can't." I slap my palm over my open mouth. "It's just — I have an appointment with a . . . my headache specialist."

"All right. Tomorrow then?" Ms Smyrnious suggests.

"Yes, that would be great." Maybe I can get Julie to show me how to divide Ned and the donkey before then.

"May I have your note, please?" Ms Smyrnious holds out her hand.

"Note?" I repeat.

"For your absence."

Just for a heartbeat I feel some panic, but then I

take a deep breath and force my shoulders back. "I'm sorry. I, like, totally forgot." I smile. Jay won't mind forging another signature for me. There's no reason to panic.

In class we're listening to the second round of presentations. I've opted out of this round, so my next project better score high. Andrea's up again, this time talking about how to take care of a horse — I guess horses are all she ever thinks about. She looks pretty dozy up there, swaying back and forth as she talks about — what is she even talking about? I tune out immediately and relax, flipping through my latest *Ms Mode* for the Beauty Horoscope. As a Leo I'm supposed to go dramatic, wear intense shades. What! But I'm a Spring. Much as I hate them, pastels are what work on me. I click my tongue in disgust. Who writes this column — do they have any fashion sense at all?

Suddenly everything's quiet, as though everything's stopped around me. Was I that loud? Is the teacher behind me, looking over my shoulder? I glance back. Nope.

"Carlos, get a glass of water," Ms Smyrnious says loudly.

I swivel back and see now that Andrea's sprawled on the floor. A beached whale. No . . . actually more like a dying sardine. She actually looks small and grey and sick. Hmph. She should get some more iron in her if she's going to diet all the time. Most girls need a supplement, according to Dr. Beauty in *Teen Fashion*.

Andrea pretty much has only one friend — one person who at least tolerates her, actually — so Ms Smyrnious makes Lauren take Andrea to the office. Too bad she fainted. I'm in a good mood and I would have given Andrea another A, whatever she said. I'm sure that girl has a way with live-stock.

At least Andrea gets to miss the rest of today's classes. I'm thinking of passing out too, in math class. I practically go into a coma I'm so bored with the x and y stuff.

The only subject that I can stand to stay con-scious in is family studies. Ms Ferris asks us to draw our idea of three different clothing looks. They can be formal, casual and fun, or any other three moods we can think about. Immediately I start sketching. I picture a long flowing gown with a dipping neckline and no back. I see long gloves and hey, some small butterfly buttons on the gloves and at the back of the neck of the dress.

"Lovely, Kim," she says as she passes. "You know, I saw something similar in my pattern book, only shorter. Tiny straps, the classic black dress. You could probably make it by the end of the term, if you put in some extra hours after school or at lunch."

Extra hours? She's a great teacher and everything, and I like the class — but staying after school? Well, that just seems a little drastic for me.

"Come have a look at the book if you get a chance." Ms Ferris wanders to the next desk.

The casual outfit I draw is a two-piece cargo pantsuit, complete with lots of big safari-style pockets on the top as well as the pants.

Then I sketch a shorts set, changing all the horrible ideas Valentino and Durkin used for their Granny Golfing set. The shorts are a younger, more flattering thigh length, with my trademark square cutout at the seam. The vest is a fringed above-the-belly-button tank top.

"Ms Ferris, I have no clue where to start," Stephanie calls out from the table over to the left of me.

What? But I'm finished already. I look over my drawings and then head for Ms Ferris's desk for the pattern book. As I pass by Lauren's table, I sneak a peek at her sketch. A stick man with a box over his body. I can't help smiling.

I grab the Simple Style book and sit down again to browse. Flipping through is almost as good as looking at a *Ms Mode*, only the models aren't real, just sketched-in bodies to fit the clothes.

Time always crawls when I'm in Ms Smyrnious's classes, but now as I get really into the fashions, redesigning and adding accessories in my head, of course the bell rings.

I return the book and Ms Ferris motions for me to look at the pattern in the book she's holding. Mmm, it is nice. I jot down the number.

"So if you get the pattern and the material, you can get started immediately," Ms Ferris tells me.

"Sure, I'll try. Only I'm awfully busy." I want to tell her about my modelling career, to really impress her, but I stop myself. It can't get back to my parents. Instead I rush off to the cafeteria to line up, buy a veggie wrap and head for my usual table.

"Hey Kimmmberly. Want to go to the mall with me?" Jay asks me as I sit down.

I pick up the veggie wrap and peer into it to make sure there's nothing weird inside. Who wants sprouts hanging from their teeth, after all? "You mean you're not grounded, for a change?" The veggie wrap seems safe so I bite in.

"My father and I reached an agreement." For a moment Jay sounds different. Hard, and sharp.

I search his face and notice a brightness in his eyes. He could be about to cry or about to laugh. But knowing him, and that he's just had something over on his dad again, I figure he must be pretty happy. I ruffle his hair a little. "Sorry, Jay. I'm going to a photo shoot with Gunther. You know, for my modelling agency."

He grins with admiration and then covers up quickly. "Gunther. Ohhh, Gunther!" He tries to imitate my voice and flips his hand with a limp wrist. "Look at me, Gunther. Take my picture." Then he gets serious again. "Want me to come?"

I shake my head. "You'll never be allowed in." I take a bite of my wrap, then push it to the side. "Here, Jay, can you sign this?" I slide over a sheet of stationery on which I've excused myself for another tension headache.

Jay loops a large signature again. "When's the photo thing?" He pushes the paper back at me and I tuck it away. "I can come and hang around outside. I don't mind."

"Right after school." I watch his eyes follow someone walking behind me now and I turn. Lauren Dreyburgh is passing with Horsewoman Andrea. I punch Jay's arm hard.

"She looks different, don't you think?" Jay asks me.

I make a face at him. "As if I care."

"Andrea's almost skinny and Lauren looks thinner too. What's with them?" Jay takes a huge bite from his hot dog and keeps talking. "Did they both catch something?"

"Shut up, Jay." I cover his mouth with my hand.

"Mmrrrough jealous."

I take my hand from his mouth, just in time to catch the last word. "Oh yes. A showroom model for Valentino and Durkin's is going to be jealous of those two losers." I roll my eyes. Inside I feel a strange new power. "If you're coming to my shoot, I don't want to see you drooling over every woman around."

"You *modelled*?" Emily asks from the table next to us.

I smile and toss my hair back.

It's already starting. And the buzz continues around school, thanks to Julie and Jay. Everyone looks at me as though I'm ten times as pretty. They whisper about me. *There goes Kimberly, did you know she's modelling now?* Even the teachers seem to look at me differently. I'm not just some stupid girl who can't handle numbers and tests. My life already seems a lot more exciting to everyone — and that was just my first assignment. It's all going to come my way. I'll never end up like my parents! No filing for me, no computers, no business casual.

And if that lame showroom disaster impresses them, wait till I win the *Ms Mode* Great Model Search. Everything will be perfect then.

End-of-the-day history class, I flip open one of Julie's magazines to the quiz. Are You Getting What You Want Out of Life?

I click my ballpoint open.

You're invited to an all night rave and your parents say no way. You:

(a) stomp off to your room, slamming the door. You're staying home this time, but they owe you.

(b) promise to say no to drugs and be home by 11, insisting they should trust you.

103

(c) help your mother with the dishes and then
    pretend to go to bed early. You'll slip out
    through your bedroom window later.

I look at the marks already on the quiz. Julie
chose (a). Of course that's the one you're supposed
to choose. If you're really dying to do something,
can you just accept no? Don't you owe it to yourself
to go for the things that are really important to
you, no matter what it takes? I chew at my pen.
Really, ticking off your choices and adding up your
score is not what the quizzes are about. They're
there to teach you things. So on to the next:

You need money for a prom dress that's way too
expensive (from your parents' point of view). You:

(a) forget it and plan a Goodwill shopping trip
    with your buds. You're bound to find
    something else that's both funky and cheap.
(b) offer to wash the car, vacuum the family room
    and clean the bathroom for a substantial
    increase in your allowance.
(c) invent a field trip and birthday gifts you need
    money for. If you do it in small frequent doses,
    your parents will never notice.

The (b) answers all seem to depend on your parents coming around and giving in, which you're
never really guaranteed. Julie ticked (a), but I personally liked (c). That's what I mean about quizzes
teaching you things. I might never have thought of
that one myself.

Your ancient aunt is visiting on a Friday night and your family expects you to stick around. Of course, you're invited to the sleepover of the year. You:

(a) plan a shopping trip that includes Auntie for another day.

(b) stick around for supper and when she falls asleep during the movie, take off for the sleepover.

(c) tell your parents you have a major school project and Friday's the only night your whole group can get together to work on it.

Julie finally shows some spark and picks (c). *Ehhhhhh!* Wrong. Her parents would probably suggest the whole group meet at their house — Auntie would love to meet the group too. I pick (b), although if it were my grandmother, I'd do the mall thing. My granny loves to buy me tons of stuff, and what's wrong with that?

Your best friend wants you to cut class to line up for Dozers tickets, a group that's not even your fave. You:

(a) pretend your parents overheard, so you can't possibly accompany your bud.

(b) talk her into waiting till after school.

(c) go along with your best bud. Girls just want to have fun.

Hmm. This one is a toughie. Julie checked off (c). I guess she really is a pretty good best friend after all — better than I am, because I feel like checking off (a).

Your major guy needs a lot of money, no questions asked. You:

(a) tell him all your money is locked up in bonds and securities. Sorry, hon.

(b) give him all your allowance and the money you made looking after that drooling mastiff over Christmas holidays. Love has no price.

(c) insist you need to know why he needs the money, then you'll gladly empty your bank account and sell your Beanie Babies collection, so long as it's for a worthwhile cause.

Julie is a major tightwad and chooses (a). For me (b) has to be the answer. Money doesn't mean anything to me now that I am a working model. Sigh! I can't help smiling a little.

So now I add up my score and flip to the answers page to see what I'm "getting out of life."

Ten to fifteen points makes you a Doormat:

Doormats tend to bend over backwards so that no one gets mad at them. Still, people wipe their feet all over you, and eventually even the person who answers "whatever" to every question will explode if they never get their way. Better to offend people sometimes and please yourself at least occasionally.

Sixteen to twenty points earns you the title of Surfer:

The Surfer likes to coast through life, sometimes leaning one way, sometimes the other. But can you keep your balance all the time, or will the next big wave crash you? Work on setting down some principles and goals that help you choose the path you really want to follow.

Twenty-one to thirty is a Bulldozer:

A Bulldozer plows through difficulties, perhaps a little stubbornly, but nevertheless you know what you want and you push for it. Be very careful that you don't come on too strong and become The Steamroller.

And thirty-one to forty is The Steamroller:

Everything that gets in your way gets mowed down and flattened. Perhaps you should deny yourself occasionally, so that the people you love still respect you.

I turn out to be a Surfer. Only I'm sure that's only temporary. My score is pretty high, almost into the next category. I have goals after all. I want an exciting life where everyone thinks I'm special and interesting. I'm planning on winning the *Ms Mode* Great Model Search, and meanwhile I'll go to that photo shoot this afternoon. Maybe better modelling jobs will come my way after. Print work must require professional photos, after all.

A Bulldozer is what I should really be in this quiz. It's the category Julie falls into, only close to the lower end. She's almost a Surfer. Our scores aren't that far apart. We really do have a lot in common. That's me and Julie, two Bulldozers . . .

They should give it a nicer name, though. A bull-dozer's not a very flattering image . . . The long-legged tanned surfer girl image suits me better, actually. Still, I need to have more in my life than what my parents have, than what they want for me. If I have to be a Bulldozer to get it, then I will. Some way, somehow. And soon, very soon, I am going to have it.

chapter 12

Jay's brother drives us to Gunther's photo studio. It turns out to be in that same warehouse district as Valentino and Durkin's. But Gunther is more what I expect from a photographer than Valentino's was for my first modelling client.

He's a small-built guy with a deep tan and blond waves. He's wearing slim-fit jeans with a black shirt open down the chest. You can see a gold chain and cross. He's gotta be a good guy with a cross, right?

But the minute he gets my name and confirms the details Elaine Chev gave him, he snarls at Jay. "Get out of here. We have to work alone."

"Can't my boyfriend sit in the other room or some—"

Gunther waves him away. "No."

Jay folds his arms across his chest and stares at Gunther. For a moment it looks like he's not going anywhere — like he's going to be a Steamroller. Then suddenly he grins and turns away. "I'll be right outside, Kim. Have fun."

How cool! Jay's at least a Bulldozer anyway. No one walks over him. "Come! Come!" Gunther tells me and I follow him through a tiny foyer into a huge high-ceilinged room. There's a lot of junk lying around — wires, lights, strange white umbrellas, a couple of stools, a fur rug, a leather couch. Even a motorcycle, of all things.

"What did you bring? Let me see." Gunther motions to my duffel bag. Then he paws through the clothes. "No high heels. Well, that's all right. I have some. But where's the glamour here?"

Exactly my point. "Actually, I thought I would go for the girl-next-door look," I explain.

"Girl-next-door, nah. What you need is sequins or feathers." Gunther continues to grope through my things, frowning. "What's this?" He holds up my red maillot. "This could work. We could build on this look." He pulls it out and tosses it to me. "Put this on with . . . let's see . . . " He rummages through a wooden box and pulls out the highest platform shoes I've ever seen. "You're a size nine? Models always have big feet."

"Size seven," I answer, hoping this will let me off the hook.

"Close enough." He pitches them at me.

"High heels with a bathing suit?" I squint at him.

"Really! You aren't going to be frolicking on the beach. It's a fashion look." Gunther rolls his eyes. "The heels give you a lovely leg. Pushes you forward slightly."

Tacky, I think. I'm still squinting.

He waves his hand. "Hurry up and change. Nobody pays a model to think."

I look to the left and the right. He can't expect me to strip right in front of him . . .

"Behind the screen over there." He answers the question I haven't dared to ask.

"Leave your clothes there, it's all right," he calls as I pull off the new capri pants I saved for this occasion. They were supposed to be my sophisticated girl-next-door look. Gunther must be watching my clothing drop from under the screen. I quickly slip the bathing suit on and adjust it. Then I step up into the ridiculous shoes and inch forward carefully.

"Lie down on the rug here and kick up your legs."

I hesitate. On the beach, wearing the skimpiest bikini doesn't bother me. But when you're the only one in the room and the other person is eyeing you . . . Suddenly Gunther reaches for me and I draw back. "Don't be a baby," he says as he grabs my hair and pulls it all to one side, over my shoulder. "On your stomach please."

I wince as I do what he says. His rug looks like it might have fleas.

Then Gunther fiddles with his lamps, bringing them forward. He positions a white umbrella behind me and then begins snapping. "Not so wooden. I need some expression. Snuggle into that rug and then lift yourself. Like so." He shows me how to use my arms as support.

Snuggle into the fleas . . . Ugh, I feel itchy all over. Plus, I feel almost undressed, and very stupid, with those huge shoes hanging from my feet.

"All right, I want a sweet smile to begin with. Nice." *Click, click!* "Pull a strand of your hair over your eyes . . . Now close them . . . You're eating a *sinfully* delicious cake . . . You're in heaven." *Click, click!* "Turn forward . . . Look directly into the camera, as though you want something *very* badly. Nice!

"All right, take it off and throw this on." He hands me a green feather boa.

"What?"

He rolls his eyes again. "Just kidding. Leave the suit on but pull the straps down and cross your arms like so."

My hands have to cover the top of the suit, and with the feathers hanging down the front, I'm not sure any of the suit even shows.

"Sit on the stool, please."

Well, at least I'm off that awful carpet.

"No! No! Not like an elephant. You'll create a line across your stomach. Lift your weight up. Perch."

It's the most uncomfortable position in the world. My legs are crossed, my toes are gripping onto my stilt shoes and I'm "perched" right on the edge.

"Look happy, dreamy, relaxed. Nice . . . nice."
Click, click, click!

Next I have to slip into a sequin dress that's really an extended tube top. Along with it I have to wear boots that almost reach the hem, they're so high. Gunther wheels over the motorcycle and asks me to straddle it. "Clients *love* this one. You may get a lot of print work in *Motorcycle Weekend* or *Wrestling Today*."

Motorcycle Weekend, Wrestling Today . . . Ew, and what about those scuzzy calendars some of the boys have hanging in their lockers? I never thought that all those women on display like that were models, professional models, just like me. I guess I really only imagined being photographed for fashion magazines.

This time I "perch" over the leather seat of the bike. *Click, click, click!* The muscles in my thighs burn from holding myself up. "Throw your head back and laugh. That's right. More abandon."

Hmph. It's hard to do abandon when I feel so uncomfortable and unclothed. I never get the chance to wear my girl-next-door outfit or my sophisticated capri pants.

Gunther simply wraps the strap around his camera and puts it down on the stool. "That's it, we're done. Do you have the money?" He scratches across his chest.

"No, no. I gave it to Ms Chev." I can't help folding my arms across the tube top sparkle so that I'm not so bare.

"Fine. In two weeks the proofs will be at Elaine's." Gunther walks away and I gather that I can change back into my street clothes.

Quickly I slip back into my shirt and capri pants. I grab my duffel bag and then hunt around for Gunther. I'm not anxious to check the door at the back so I just call out, "Um . . . thanks. See you." My voice sounds a bit shaky.

Walking towards the door in my own shoes, I feel a bit more in contact with solid ground. Only inside I feel different. The shoot didn't go anything the way I imagined. No applause, no cheers. A couple of "Nice!" comments tossed my way, but mostly it was only greyness. It's as though those pink bubbles have all popped, and now my insides are coated with a soapy stickiness I just want to shower and get rid of, plus I still feel itchy all over. Stupid rug.

As I step out of the foyer I can't see Jay anymore. I check my watch and see that the shoot has taken close to two hours. I can't blame him, really. I wouldn't wait that long with nothing to do. He must've left.

Suddenly hands close over my eyes. I scream and elbow whoever it is in the guts.

"Ow! Hey, it's me!"

Too late I turn and see Jay. He barely manages

to hold on to a brown bag in his hand as he doubles over. "I . . . bought . . . you a . . . drink . . . and a chocolate bar," he gasps as he tries to get back some breath.

"I'm so sorry!" I can't help myself — it's so terrific to have him there, I throw my arms around him and touch my lips to his cheek.

"Hey!" He turns a little so his lips are near mine. "That's much better," he whispers. Then even though it wasn't in the How to Make Your Hottie Pant guideline, I let him kiss me.

chapter 13

Instead of calling a cab, I want to walk and get rid of the scummy feeling of the photo shoot.

"Just how bad was it?" Jay asks after we've gone about six blocks.

"Well, it's not like he hit on me or anything. But the poses he put me in, and the clothes he wanted me to wear, seemed so sleazy. And maybe if the studio had some zip or sparkle to it, or if the clothes he loaned me weren't old and worn . . . Maybe it would have felt more — I don't know — glamorous. But it just felt . . . low." I shudder, thinking about Gunther and his camera snapping away. Jay stops walking, pulls me towards him and hugs me.

Instead of feeling better, I hear my voice crack. "What if it's all like that, Jay? I thought modelling was the most exciting job in the world. Maybe it's just low and scummy . . . and boring." I start to cry now.

He continues hugging, saying nothing for a while. "Nah," he finally says. "You've got that *Ms Mode* contest coming up. I bet those babes don't put up with old clothes and dirty studios. You just have to hang in, Kim. Come on, it's not always gonna be like this." He pats my back.

And then we kiss again and I start to feel better. Jay's right. Maybe this modelling agency thing is bottom-feeder stuff. Maybe Gunther is just a third-rate photographer and Valentino and Durkin's a two-bit rag company. But *Ms Mode* — *that's* going to be different. When I get chosen in the *Ms Mode* search, there won't be anything third-rate or two-bit about it.

We walk all the way to a bus stop closer to the office district, and then wait there to catch one.

When I get home, I promise myself, I'm going to take a long hot bath with a ton of bath oil and a stack of my magazines. There's nothing better for putting glamour back in a person's life. If only I could stay in the tub forever.

Tuesday there's no more putting off my make-up math quiz. Ms Smyrnious accepts no excuses and writes my name on the board along with the time: 3:30. So I corner Stephanie during our spare to get some last-minute pointers. Lauren and the other loner, Andrea, are sitting with her, but I pay no attention to them.

Stephanie quickly shows me how to divide fractions. It involves switching around the numerator and denominator on the divisor so that the donkey actually rides Ned. And then you multiply the first fraction by this new odd riding couple. Makes no sense to me, but I can memorize it for an afternoon and then at least I'll get the fraction questions right.

The x and y problems still baffle me. I can't help thinking about my modelling at Valentino and Durkin's. I was there at 11:00, at $25 an hour, and I finished at 4:00. That made 5 times $25 which is $125. Then I have to pay Ms Chev 20% which is ... $25. That means I earn $100 ... but then I still need another $100 just to make the $200 to cover my session with Gunther. I figure this all out with a calculator, no stupid x's or y's involved. But Ms Smyrnious insists we show our work and that means using the letters the way she taught us — well, those of us who understood it.

In family studies, Ms Ferris manages to cheer me up just a little. She hands me the pattern for the dress she showed me the other day. "Size five, I presume?"

"Yes! How did you know?" I carefully open the thick envelope.

"Remember we took measurements back before the boxer shorts project? I went ahead and bought the pattern, knowing how busy you are." She winks at me. "And I have this fabric remnant that I thought might work, if you want to go with black."

I touch the material. It's smooth with just a touch of sheen to it. "It's beautiful."

"Good. Then start by reading the instructions

and cutting apart the pattern pieces you need."

I breeze through the instructions and unfold the pieces, smoothing the folded tissue with my hand. In my mind I'm adding a square slit on either side of the dress already. I do end up staying about half of my lunch hour, till Ms Ferris herself has to leave.

But the rest of the lunch I spend with Julie, and I depress myself all over again telling her about my experiences with Gunther. Only she doesn't seem to understand how bad it was.

"So you don't want to be in a motorcycle ad." She shrugs "C'mon, Kim. All great models have to start somewhere. I'd do anything if it meant a break in my photography career. What kind of camera did he use anyway?" Miss Future–Photo-Journalist/Bulldozer quizzes me some more about Gunther's equipment and the studio. The details about the awful outfits, the scuzzy poses and flea-bitten rug all fly right over her. She doesn't seem to believe any of the shoot was that bad. The more I tell her, the worse I feel. Where's Jay when you need him?

And the buzz about me modelling continues around the school. It's like one of those pink bubbles inside me has escaped and blown up into this huge unreal thing, just waiting for everyone to find out how small-time I am. How I'm really not beautiful enough to be one of the chosen few, like the supermodels I have tacked in the photo frame on my desk at home. How I'm afraid that big hollow bubble will break, leaving soapy scum everywhere.

Talk about depressing. After school I sit alone at the front of the classroom with Ms Smyrnious scribbling away at some papers on her desk. The hands on the wall clock tick slowly around, but not slowly enough. Because I have to work backwards showing my work à la Smyrnious method, I don't finish the test in time. She insists I wait as she corrects it right then and there.

So I have to sit and watch her. Her lips get all kinds of exercise as she goes through my answers. The outside corners of her mouth go down together, and then they straighten. Then only the left side tugs downward. Now the two lips do push-ups against each other. "Hmm," she finally says as she slides the test towards me.

A red number, 62%, sits at the top of the page. I'm pretty happy I passed. Maybe it's a squeaker, but I don't have to show it to my parents or anything.

Wrong. Ms Smyrnious tells me I need to have one of them sign the test.

"You really should come in at lunch for extra help," she adds. "This work is the foundation for the algebra that you will use in high school."

I do some mouth exercises of my own. "I'll think

about it, Ms Smyrnious." High school? If only I could miss that experience totally. *The Great Model Search,* I think instead as I cross my fingers behind my back. Do the winners ever really go back to school after? I don't think so. It's my best hope. "Thanks, Ms Smyrnious."

"See you tomorrow, Kimberly."

I smile and nod, then head out of the room. During the car ride home, Julie invites me over to her house, but I'm feeling too stressed to go. My shoulders are all bunched up, I'm worrying about getting Mom to sign my test without Dad knowing. Hey, what's the big deal? I suddenly realize. One more big loopy signature of Jay's, that's all it will take. And I can avoid one of Dad's big rants about the importance of math and school in my future. I don't think I could stand one of those right now. Jay won't mind helping me out again. I shrug my shoulders and they relax a little.

We turn into my driveway and I wave goodbye to Julie as I climb out of the car. Before I can even unlock the house door, though, I hear the telephone ring. "Coming, coming," I mumble as I turn the key and push open the door. *Ring! Ring! Ring!* I fling my books on my bed as I track down the portable phone to my room, in time to beat the answering machine.

"May I speak to Kimberly Rainer, please?" It's Elaine Chev's voice. I'm not really ready to talk to her. I mean, does she have another job for me in another seedy garment factory already?

I swallow. "Speaking."

"Well hello, Kim. How are you?"

I picture her French manicure rapping across the desk as she waits for me to answer. "Pretty good," I lie to her.

"Good. Because I have something really exciting for you. Are you free next Wednesday?"

"Next Wednesday?" I ask weakly.

"Yes. It's an open call and I realize this will take you out of school again," she rushes out her words quickly. I can tell she really is excited. "But Detel and Company — they're the owners of many of the major malls in the area — are looking for a young person to portray Barbie on weekends and through the summer. It's a terrific opportunity. Plus, the timing works for you — if you get this job, you won't have to miss school at all. At least, after Wednesday."

"Barbie?" Now I'm excited.

"Yes. Do you want me to speak to your mother about all this?"

"N . . . No, she's at work. Um . . . "

"They want someone five-eight or over, long legs, long hair, clear skin, bright eyes, girl next door. Sounds like you, doesn't it?"

I glance over at my fashion model Barbies sitting in their places on the shelves. I can represent them. I can *be* Barbie. I smile. "Yes, it sounds exactly like me."

"Mmm, what colour is your hair again? They're leaning towards a blonde on this one."

Oh great, my best feature and this time it's going to work against me. "Well, it's kind of a cinnamon brown colour . . . " I chew at a fingernail.

"Brown, mmm . . . you wouldn't think of adjusting the colour?"

Never, never, never. But my Barbies all stare at me blankly, their lips almost pouting. They can't move or talk for themselves. They need me. "Of course I can change the shade," I tell Ms Chev.

"Good. So I don't need to speak to your mom. Do you have a pencil and paper handy for the address?"

"We always keep a pad and pen by the phone," I tell her and then take down all the details. This time the building is right next door to my father's office. Life would be so easy if I could just tell him. He could call the school for me, write the note, drop me off, maybe even take me to lunch after. Should I tell him? Would he understand about how much this chance means to me? Just this once would he let school take a back seat to my real life? Never mind that I have to dye my hair for the opportunity.

I remember back to when I last "opened the lines of communication" with him. "No way, no how, no daughter of mine!" he'd said. Well, that settles it. I just can't take the risk with my father, on something this important to me.

chapter 14

"You're going to change your hair colour!" Julie explodes over the telephone line.

I chew at a different nail, the bitter taste of the Bite-stop growing on me by now. Well, people drink black coffee and beer and eat fish eggs and calf brains and all sorts of things. Tell me they're born liking those tastes. "I'm just adjusting my hair shade slightly for this job," I explain. "Come on, Julie, I really need you to help me out on this one. Can I sleep over next Tuesday night so I don't have to tell my parents till after the interview?"

"What makes you think my mother will go for a school-night sleepover any more than yours will?"

"Drat. You're right." I think quickly. "I know — we have a group project that we have to work on together and . . . and we've left it to the last minute. It might be an all-nighter."

I hear her huffing and grumbling on the other end.

"C'mon, Julie, you're the creative one. You can fill in the blanks, make her believe it."

"Okay fine." She sighs. "I'll come up with something."

"Thanks, Julie. You're a real friend."

I have a whole week to agonize over my clothes for the audition. Barbie is a versatile woman with so many images, but I decide the day before that the look of the classic Fifties doll is the way I want to go. I fold up my capri pants — they used to call them pedal pushers back then — and a sky blue angora sweater in some tissue paper I have saved for just such an occasion. 20 Tips for Wrinkle-Free Packing gave me the hint: the tissue paper will help keep my clothes crease-free. I really do learn a lot from my fashion magazines. My dad just doesn't realize it. I lay the clothes gently in a small overnight suitcase, roll up some pyjamas and underwear and stuff them along the sides. I can't decide on my make-up so I bring my entire vanity box, throwing in my toothbrush and some accessories too.

All this is awkward to carry on the bus, and even worse to drag into the mall. My mother offered to drive it over later, but I don't want her to see what it is I've packed — or show up just as we're dying my hair. "I can't browse today with all this stuff," I tell Julie when we meet at the water fountain.

"Should have bought the dye on the weekend," she clucks.

"Yeah, well if Mom saw it and asked questions . . . "

"You're just being paranoid. She wouldn't have even noticed. Well, should we go to Economart? They've got the biggest beauty section."

I sigh. Economart's a store I usually wouldn't be caught breathing in. Their fashion selection looks like it comes straight from Valentino and Durkin's line, all rayons and polyesters in golfing grandmother colours. And the selections they do have, they pile warehouse-ceiling high. But they have at least two aisles of hair-care supplies. "I guess you're right. Economart it is."

We have to walk through what seems like aisle after aisle of plasticware, mops, brooms, small appliances, cheap electronics. My suitcase bumps against my knee as I hurry down the aisles, hoping not to be seen.

Over in the electronics section there's a familiar blond head bent over the CDs. Just for a little while I wouldn't mind having that shade of hair, I think. Jay's hair colour. I smile.

"Kimmmberly, imagine you shopping here," he teases when he sees me.

I roll my eyes at him. "We're . . . like . . . shopping for hair dye, okay, so don't make a big deal about it."

He just grins at me as he starts to tag along. But he's good about it, no more cracks. And he makes himself useful. When we get to the stacks of little hair colour boxes, he reads the instructions and compares all the colours just like us, fingering the strands of different acrylic hair samples hanging in front. "None of them are as nice as your colour, Kim."

I frown down at Number 78, Midnight Sun. Then I pull my hair forward so that I can see my own colour. Jay's right, my shade is prettier. Still, Midnight Sun looks more like a true Barbie colour.

"That's the one," Julie agrees. She picks up the package for me, seeing as I'm carrying my bags.

"You paying for it?" Jay asks in a surprised tone.

I shake my head at him. "You're too much. Of course I'm paying for it."

"Come on. I'll pocket it for you. Save your money." He's already looking left and right as he reaches for the box. "We just have to watch . . . There's the security shopper over there."

He points to a tall bulky-looking woman, some-one familiar to me.

My heart races, I'm so tempted. I could save at least the ten dollars the hair dye will cost. Jay can do this for me, I know it. And I need his help. I've already taken three hundred dollars out of my account, and it's almost all gone.

"That's Lauren's sister, isn't it?" Julie asks.

"Patricia?" I repeat. I remember her from when I was in kindergarten and she was the grade eight student who supervised us on rainy day recesses.

"Shh!" Jay gives us an annoyed raise of his eyebrows. "I can't do my work this way."

Patricia had been nice to me when my headaches started. She'd take me to the office and put cool cloths on my forehead. I don't want to make trouble for her. "That's okay, Jay. I really appreciate the offer, though." I flick my hair towards the exit cashiers and Julie leads the way.

She heads through the toy department and suddenly, peeking down the doll aisle, I see stacks of Barbies in bright fuchsia-coloured boxes. "Pink!" I say out loud.

"Hmm?" Julie turns to me.

"Look at the Barbies down there. Pink is the colour I should be wearing tomorrow!"

Julie glances down the doll aisle. "You're right. Did you bring anything?"

I shake my head. "Would pink go with this hair colour?"

"I see your point." Julie frowns. "Pink's never been my shade either. So I guess we have some serious shopping to do."

"Not with this stuff." I lift my bags slightly. "Let's find a locker."

I pay for the hair colour and the three of us walk to the customer service where I trade the sleepover gear for a tag. "Great, we're all set."

"Well, much as I want to watch you try clothes on, no way the clerks will let me hang around the changing rooms, so I'll catch you later." Jay leans over to me and I figure I've made him pant long enough. I kiss him first.

"Mmm. Good luck, Kimmm."

"You're so lucky," Julie tells me as we watch Jay take off. Then she turns to me. "Where should we start?"

"The bank," I answer. "Four dollars is not enough to do a Barbie makeover."

We do the usual line-up for the teller routine and I start to wonder if I can't get one of those bank cards without permission from my parents. Finally I hand the teller my withdrawal slip and as usual she doesn't blink an eye. "When I'm Barbie, I'll for sure be able to cover all these withdrawals," I tell Julie as I count out two hundred dollars.

"Easily," she answers. "And we're talking your future here. Money just can not be an obstacle."

It's all become pretty easy. Instead, the tough part turns out to be shopping for a pink ensemble. Normally I'll hold up anything I like near my face and hair to make sure it highlights my colouring. But popsicle pink and cinnamon brown just never complement each other even in the best of lighting. "Too bad I can't do my hair and then shop," I complain to Julie.

"Pull your hair back from your face. Maybe we can cover it with something," she suggests.

"You're brilliant." So the first thing I buy is a

pink scarf that I wrap around my head, turban-style. Then everything snaps into place and we shop for a look and a nice fit. We find a soft pink sweater set and a matching mini. I pick up some pantyhose and then some terrific white shoes with a tiny pink butterfly sitting just at the front.

When we finally head for Julie's house I'm certain that I have the perfect Barbie wardrobe, but I'm down to my last ten dollars again.

My grandmother always dyes and perms her hair and it looks and feels like burnt straw. I promise myself each time I fix it for her that I will never do that to my own hair. Still, the moment we get back to Julie's we barricade ourselves in her bathroom and rip open the hair dye box. Quickly we skim the instructions.

"We don't have time for the strand test," Julie warns me.

"Do you think anybody does?" I ask. You're supposed to take a piece of your hair, somewhere where it's not so noticeable, and leave the solution on twenty minutes just to see what happens. I chew my lip for a moment as I give my hair one last look in the mirror. "Never mind. Let's just do all of it."

"All right!" Julie cheers and starts shaking the little brown bottle. I lean back over the tub and in a moment I feel a cold trickle down my neck. After another moment the smell of bleach makes my eyes water.

"Ew, yuck, that stuff stinks. Can that be good for your hair?" Julie waves her hand in front of her nose.

"Of course. Look at what it says on the package. 'Conditions while it colours. Leaves your hair silky and soft.'" I squeeze my eyes tight against the burning odour. "Just make sure you cover all the hair."

The colour needs to set for half an hour so we spread homework around the floor just in case Julie's mom comes in. I also make Julie get her only Barbie out of the closet for inspiration. She's naked and Julie has to reattach her head — not very inspiring. "Don't you have anything for her to wear?" I ask.

She shakes her head.

"Well, give me a sock at least," I tell her, and then I tuck the abused doll into the white tennis anklet Julie hands me. The smell of my hair and the faint ballpoint moustache on Julie's Barbie depresses me. I feel a headache coming on. Still, we flip through old magazines and I find the one quiz that can cheer me up, one that I'm sure to score pretty well on: What's Your Beauty Quotient?

chapter 15

I breeze through the eye make-up section, no problem. Yes, I know that using petroleum jelly on your eyelashes and curling them can make them look just as good as if you brush on mascara. And in a pool the petroleum jelly won't run. I understand about using a lighter shadow closer to the brow and about brushing your eyebrows and only plucking them after you've taken a hot shower to open the pores.

Skin and lip make-up I'm an expert on. A light base coat under foundation hides imperfections. Lipsticks with moisturizers are a must for lips subjected to central heating. In the summer a lipstick should have sunscreen in it. Licking your lips dries them out. And I know the other stuff too. You're never supposed to use a deodorant soap on your face. Drinking at least eight glasses of water helps your skin stay healthy.

Then I hit the hair care section. Most of that I breeze through too. Hair should be trimmed every six to eight weeks to get rid of split ends. Blow-drying from the roots out increases volume. Conditioning at least once a week keeps hair healthy and prevents damage. But here's where it starts to get scary. Apparently, static hair occurs when water level in the air drops below fifty percent. So then colouring hair, especially lightening it with a product that contains peroxide, contributes not only to hair damage and dryness, but staticky hair.

Adding up all the (a), (b) and (c) answer points, I score ninety percent on the quiz, making me a Beauty Goddess. I can give counselling sessions to other teens and advise them on their beauty problems, the magazine suggests. Fine, I know all the stuff, but with my own hair I didn't practise it.

I panic now, and grab the empty hair dye box. Of course it contains peroxide. My hair is my best feature — what have I done? Condemned myself to haystack hair like my grandma?

I shake Julie's shoulder. "Let's rinse it off right now!"

"Why, is the stuff bothering your scalp?"

To make things worse, at that exact moment I do suddenly feel an uncomfortable stinging. "Yeah, let's hurry!"

We rush back to the bathroom and I lean backwards over the tub again, the cold porcelain digging at my neck. From the corner of my eye I can see the murky pink water running from my hair as Julie sprays off the dye with her shower hose. Then she shampoos in the tiny bag of conditioner.

"Do you have any other extra-strength leave-in conditioner?"

Julie frowns as she shuffles through the various plastic bottles lined up against the bathroom wall. She checks her medicine cabinet next and then in the cupboard under the sink. "Nope, none." She eyes me sitting on the tub edge now, plastic bag around my head. "I was just reading about natural beauty treatments though. Apparently olive oil or mayonnaise left in the hair overnight acts as a great conditioning treatment."

Food in my hair? I make a face, but I'm just desperate enough to try it. We head for the kitchen. It takes all of what's left in the jar in Julie's fridge to turn my head into potato salad. We both apply honey oatmeal masks too, so that my hair experiment is a little less obvious when her mother gets in.

But we really shouldn't have bothered. Her mother doesn't even blink when she comes in and sees us covered in goo. "Don't worry, things will all work out, dear," she tells me with a hug. "You're always welcome at this house."

"Uh, thanks." It seems a strange comment on our beauty packs. I mean, just how bad do we look? On the way back to Julie's room I nudge her with my elbow. "What's your mother talking about?"

"Oh well, that lame story about a last-minute project would never have washed. So I told her your parents were splitting up. That this was a bad time for you, what with them fighting and screaming . . . "

"But Julie, my parents don't even argue! Well, sometimes, over stupid little things . . . " Terminal boredom, that's their real problem, I think. That and the fact that they want me to be just like them.

"Don't worry about it." Julie cuts into my train of thought. "In a couple of days I'll tell Mom that they're back together again. She'll feel really happy about that, and it's not something she'd mention to either of your parents at the grocery check-out or anything."

We're back in her room now and I see Julie's sad Barbie lying wide-eyed in her sock sleeping bag. Where was Ken when you needed him? Now I can't help thinking about Jay's dad standing at the bank machine by that woman who wasn't Jay's mother. "Are Mr. and Mrs. Friessen separating?" I ask.

"I don't think so. My cousin goes to Mapleview High. She told me the principal is pretty popular with everyone — ladies included — but I haven't heard anything more than that. You?"

I shake my head.

Julie reaches over and tugs some of my hair from under the plastic bag. "Don't you want to rinse all this guck out and see what colour your hair is now?"

"Dying to. But for maximum conditioning, I'm

leaving it on till tomorrow morning, just like the article said."

We wash off our sticky faces, though, and my skin feels smooth and soft. I'm crossing my fingers my hair will feel the same when I finally rinse it.

"If it's really bad, I'll tie it back in a ponytail and wrap the pink scarf around it," I tell Julie next morning when I finally get out of the shower. My hair looks as healthy as always so far, but I throw up my hands when Julie offers me a blow dryer. "No, no! It'll dry it out! All that mayonnaise will have gone to waste." Instead I towel my hair and gently run a comb through it.

As I get dressed we watch my hair develop like one of those instant photographs. I keep checking it in the mirror. And the most amazing thing happens. My colour changes beautifully. The cinnamon brown tone lightens perfectly to reflect the shade of my outfit. Not only is my hair silky and manageable but it's now a dark blond. The perfect shade for Barbie.

"Do you have scissors and some needle and thread?" I ask Julie.

She brings a sewing kit from the kitchen and I go to work. The pink scarf turns into a hair band and with the snippits of pink cloth I have left, I quickly handstitch a shift for Julie's abused Barbie.

Make-up, make-up, I think as I stare at Barbie's ballpoint-stained face. Her eyes are an aqua blue and mine are more a grey blue, depending on what I'm wearing. I flip through my vanity case and choose a sparkle blue powder for my lids, and Sapphire Blue to line them with. Classic frosted pink is the shade of lipstick I use. Julie's Barbie only sports holes where her earrings used to be, but I fumble for a little velvet sack I stashed in with my make-up last night. There it is. I pull out some button pearls my grandma gave me at Christmas.

"One sec." Julie holds up a finger. "I have just the finishing touch." She takes something from her dresser top — a powder puff. "For your head. Can I?"

I nod, and she dusts my hair with something that looks like miniature diamonds. Barbie really is the modern day princess girl. I smile.

"They've *got* to pick you," Julie says as I stare at myself in her full-length mirror. "Let me take a picture." She takes her camera from a bag in the closet and clicks away.

I do feel like that princess. Suddenly this one appointment becomes more important than the *Ms Mode* search. Only it's getting late. The open call starts at nine and I'm supposed to arrive at least fifteen minutes before.

Julie's mom takes us to school a little early for

some other project we've made up. Then I'm too nervous to find a phone booth and call a cab, so I catch a bus.

What are the odds, the bus drives right alongside a grey Chevy Cavalier. It can't be, can it? Other people drive horrible little econo-boxes too. The driver turns for a second, though, and I see — yes, it is. My father.

I duck my head and scramble for the seat across the aisle, just to be a little farther from that window. Everything feels hot and rushed inside me. I start to chew the nail on my baby finger and then stop myself and breathe deeply. It's okay, I tell myself as I watch the Cavalier scoot ahead. A bus is much slower than a car, and besides, Dad parks in a lot underneath his building. He won't see me get off and head for the building next door.

Still, as I get off I slink like a criminal into the complex. I hate that. I need to make powerful strides, push my hips forward, throw my shoulders back and be confident — Model Barbie, that's me. And then I take another deep breath and force myself to be exactly that. Suddenly I forget Dad and feel all roller-coaster excited.

One more pathetic detail to look after, though. I search the lobby for a pay phone and dial my school. "Um, yes, hello. It's Mrs. Rainer, speaking. Kimberly Rainer in 7-A will be absent today . . . Pardon? Oh, she has a cold, as I do." Now I cough.

"Thank you. We'll try. Probably tomorrow. Thanks again."

Now I can really enjoy the bubbles floating up inside me. Everything's taken care of.

chapter 16

Detel and Company's office sits on the twenty-second floor of the building, and there's a crowd of people milling around the only four elevators that go that high. As I get closer I see that the crowd is entirely made up of girls. Tall girls with long legs, swinging hair in all shades, clear skin and large white smiles. It's as though a whole department store full of Barbies have come to life.

There's a soft *ding* and the doors of one elevator slide open. The Barbies suddenly rush towards it, pushing at each other. Another *ding* and part of the crowd heads towards another opening elevator. Still they all don't fit in, and I join the slower left-over bunch.

I'm not great at small talk, but I give the five leftover girls my best smile. Only one smiles back. The rest kind of stare at me with narrowed eyes.

As we wait I can't help but give them my own Barbie test. The girl that smiled obviously has good personality, only she's shorter than me by a head. I check out her feet and she's already wearing really high heels. There's no way she can be the five-foot-eight the company asked for.

Of the other four, one has bright orange hair and tons of freckles, and three have dark hair. With my hair and eye colouring, I'm the only real Barbie contender here. But some of them are carrying portfolio cases.

"Didn't you bring your portfolio?" the short smiley one asks me as we step into the elevator.

"No, no. Mine's not even ready. Were we supposed to?" I ask.

She just smiles as she raises and drops one shoulder.

"Aren't you too short?" One of the taller dark-haired ones asks her. I notice now she also has dark skin. Oh my gosh, it's Nina.

"My agent says I have The Look and they won't even notice my height once they see me in person." Again she smiles, but she also does this little head toss. Maybe she doesn't have such a great personality after all.

Another dark-haired girl turns to Nina. "No offence or anything, but aren't you the wrong colour for Barbie?"

"Aren't your eyebrows a little thick?" Nina comes back. "Let's face it, ladies, the real Barbie is over forty years old. Any one of us looks way better. It's going to just depend on the interviewer's mood. Almost none of us has exactly the traditional Barbie features."

Almost no one. I actually do — my face and hair,

at least. Nobody has Barbie's hourglass figure. Suddenly the other girls all stare at me as though checking for a flaw. Luckily the bell dings again and it's our floor.

We join a line leading to a receptionist's desk and wait for further instructions. I see everyone else madly scribbling out some form, so I'm guessing I'll get one of those too.

"Anybody got a pen?" somebody pleads.

"Yup," another girl answers, but then just grins and doesn't offer one.

The first girl tries to get back to the receptionist to borrow something to write with, but meets the nasty looks of the line waiting.

"Here," I tell her, handing her an old chewed-up stick pen. What can it hurt? This girl is too plump to be Barbie.

Finally I get my sheet of paper, which turns out to be an application form. I fill it out carefully in my best handwriting. Everything Barbie does should be pretty, I think.

About half of the form is very easy: name, address, school, interests, experience. But in the end there's something like an essay question: What would it mean to you to be Barbie?

Ack, writing — it's like schoolwork! My brain freezes. But this is too important, I have to think of something. I see a fashion magazine lying on a rack against the wall. One of the headlines reads

How to Tell if He's Husband Material. That's it. I have to imagine the quiz, How to Tell if You're the Perfect Barbie.

I look like her — wouldn't that score the most points? I mean, Barbie sits on a shelf. Usually, with her high heels, she can't even stand on her own, and she just needs to look good. Her biggest problem is choosing which outfit to wear. Aha — better answer! I think. I'm really good at accessorizing!

Hmm, maybe not. I stare at the magazine with the husband quiz again. Finally I walk over and pick it up, flipping to the quiz to pick up some clues. The questions deal mostly with how a guy treats other people, how often he calls his mother, whether he brings flowers to dinner.

How does Barbie treat other people? She's awfully cool, with just a tiny smile, but I'm sure she would never have elbowed others out of the way to grab the first elevator. I glance around.

Finally I write:

Barbie is everything that a little girl
wants to become. She's healthy and
glamorous, with beautiful clothes. She enjoys
a wide variety of activities and yet manages
to have a really nice boyfriend, Ken. I think I
could be Barbie, not only because I look like
her and have good fashion sense, but also

because I can be the kind of friend Barbie
has become to millions of little girls.

I smile. I really like that last one. I turn my
application in and the receptionist tells me to take
a seat.

Six girls go in at the same time. They leave.
Another six go in. None look particularly excited or
disappointed when they come out, so I'm sure they
aren't told anything. Another set of six passes in
and out, and then another.

Finally, after an hour and a half wait, I get to go
in with Nina and the other last-elevator Barbies.
There are two men sitting behind a desk, and a
woman standing by a tripod.

"Would you kindly line up over there, please?"
She hands each of us a number on a piece of yellow
paper and tells us to hold it up as she takes our picture.

Just as the photographer peers into the camera,
the freckled tall Barbie kind of leans towards the
short smiley one and then actually rests her elbow
on top of Smiley's head. She does this like it's the
most natural thing in the world, but anyone watching can't help realizing just how short Smiley is.

And Smiley Barbie looks like she's ready to kill
Freckle-face. The flash goes off with that killer-
instinct look written all over her girl-next-door
face.

The men take turns asking us questions. "How are you doing in school?" one asks Smiley Shorty Barbie.

"I'm an honour student and I'm on the cheerleading squad."

I give her high points for that one. Still, with that look of murder on her face — captured forever on film — I'm sure they can't choose her.

"How do you think having a live Barbie will affect children who visit the toy department?"

"It will be great. They'll think it's magic, like the tooth fairy or something. They'll believe in dreams come true. I know my dream will come true if you choose me to be your ambassador of goodwill."

Smiley Shorty's giving the right answers, I can tell. I try to learn from her. Freckle-face Barbie does even better because she talks about her volunteer work at the children's hospital.

Dark-haired Barbie Number 1 tells about her position on school council and her athletic trophies. Only I notice she has a really low hairline. She's pretty enough, but there's only a narrow band between her really thick eyebrows and her hair, making her look like Cavewoman Barbie.

Dark-haired Barbie Number 2 sports a small skull tattoo on her left shoulder. Do the judges notice? If I do, *they* must, I decide. Plus her teeth aren't quite right. Her two incisors hang a bit long, like fangs. Werewolf Barbie. It would be enough to give a little girl nightmares.

Nina is up next. She's nothing like the plastic princess of fashion. She wears a bright emerald pantsuit that matches her flashing green eyes. The sides of her hair are done in bunches of little braids and jangley gold earrings and bracelets hang from her ears and wrists. She flashes a huge white-toothed smile. They ask her the standard questions and finish with how she feels she represents the true ideals of Barbie. "Well, I think the demographics of the area served by Detel and Company Malls will show a large visible minority population. Little girls might like to see themselves reflected in Barbie, and I can act as a positive role model."

The judges scribble furiously on their clipboards. Brainy Brown Barbie, maybe.

Now they look up at me. "How are your school grades?"

I try not to frown. "Well, I'm getting an A+ in family studies, largely because of my fashion designs."

"What are your out-of-school interests?"

I know the right answer to this one. It's got to be: In my spare time I like to work with handicapped children. For a split second I wonder if they will check on our answers. I mean, if not, I can say *anything*, right? I chew on the inside of my lip and decide I better give them the truth. "I own five Barbies myself and I like to design and sew clothes for them. Um, I also really enjoy reading fashion magazines."

"And how do you see yourself embodying the true characteristics of Barbie?"

"I look like her." I smile at the two men sitting behind the desks, then turn towards the woman standing at the camera. "I think I have the right fashion flair. Plus I just love Barbie. I know how all those little girls coming to see live Barbie feel." I glance back at the men. Nobody's taking down any notes. Desperation time, that's what this is — not the time to play cool. I take a deep breath. *Eye contact,* I think, from our presentation tips in Ms Smyrnious's class. I look first into one pair of eyes, and then another, then I turn to the photographer again. "I'd work really hard to be the best representative that I could." A dramatic pause and another smile. "I really want to be your Barbie."

I stop then, thinking it's got to be enough. Anymore and I'll start tripping over my tongue. And let's face it, Barbie's not a woman of many words.

The woman behind the camera smiles back and I think, Yesss I've got the job! "Thank you," one of the men tells us. "We'll make our decision tomorrow and call you tomorrow evening. Our new Barbie will be making a grand entrance at the Fairview Mall this Saturday. Any of you ladies not available this Saturday?"

"No problem for me," I say, and I gather it's what everyone else says in their own way. There's a general enthusiastic murmuring.

"Great, would you tell the next group to come in?"

I make a graceful sweep out the door just in case the judges are still watching. Of the last-elevator girls, I feel sure I'm the best one. Only the girls we face as we step out the door are a whole new batch of beautiful Barbies.

chapter 17

I got away with it! It wasn't that hard, I think, as I turn in my absentee letter next day to Ms Smyrnious. The closest brush I had was when I'd left the Detel building and nearly bumped into Dad. He must have been on his coffee break, since he was carrying a bag and a cup in his hand. Luckily, my father exists only in the world of work and computers. The rest of his life he walks through as if he's an alien — a brain-dead one at that. He stared right at me but didn't even blink. He's so in another world. I just walked around him to the bus stop.

In class I try hard to tune in to what Smyrnious is teaching today — just in case. Nobody wants Barbie to be failing math or English. I copy all the math examples down from the board, following her step by step.

Only I notice Jay whispering to Carlos and then giving Lauren a big smile. Why does he bother with her? I want to scream at him: *I'm* the pretty one. Pay attention to me.

They're all chuckling now — must be some kind of joke. She's a funny one all right. Ms Smyrnious tells them to settle down now.

Already I'm starting to get lost with this algebra equation. Every operation turns into a sharp corner that my brain bangs into. Confused, stupid, I can't wade through the maze. My breath gets quicker. I feel a pounding start behind my eyes. But I refuse to get another headache over math.

So I take a deep breath and I force myself to think about happier, exciting things. I picture myself as Barbie, aloof and beautiful with a jewelled tiara on my head. *Tonight, I'll find out for sure.* The figures on the board fade. Then I see myself as Barbie/*Ms Mode* model of the year. The board and Ms Smyrnious disappear altogether. I stand on a runway and hear applause just like the good part of my dream. And I know that if I'm chosen for either of those jobs, everything will come my way. No more stupid school or homework lectures. No more talk about college and my future. No dead-end jobs like my parents. How can Jay look at anyone else but me then?

My mind only comes back to the classroom when we switch to language arts. The presentations finally done and over with, we begin a new unit: media. Smyrnious tries to start a discussion on the effects of TV, film, newspapers and magazine on the public.

It's amazing. She calls on Andrea, Ms Heavyweight Browner of the entire school. Only Andrea's changed. She really isn't fat anymore. In fact, she's thin. And dazed-looking. Seems like her head is empty too. She says absolutely nothing to Smyrnious. Not "I don't know" or "I need to think about that." She doesn't smile or shake her head. It's great to watch the brainer turn lame.

Her only bud, Lauren, jumps in to save her. "I think the media only give us extremes. We don't like to read or watch normal average stuff — it's just not interesting. So they show the most awful and violent things going on in the world, or the most beautiful perfect things. Take women, for example, and their body image. They see these exceptional-looking models and actresses whose faults are airbrushed away. Then ordinary women constantly diet, exercise, shave, tweeze, cream, cover and make themselves over — anything to look like something they can never be."

"Oh, come on." I don't mean to join in, but Lauren makes me mad. "I like seeing beautiful people on TV and in magazines. And people want to make their lives better in all kinds of other ways. They want to know how to garden or decorate their homes. They want to put on make-up and fix their hair. Yeah, and eat and exercise better too."

Lauren argues back that being thinner or more made up doesn't mean someone is better looking. That the media tells us what's beautiful, so we'll spend all our money to try to become that type of beauty.

"But what about the decorating and gardening?" I snap back at her.

"It's all part of the lie: That you can have a perfect body, perfect garden, perfect house, perfect job. It's the perfect lie." There's no way I can change her mind, I think. She's just annoying. Instead I cross my arms and let the others in the class carry on the discussion.

Carlos calls out how he likes girls "built for comfort," and Jay agrees.

"Girls are not built for anything," Lauren snaps at them. "We're not furniture or houses." The girls in the class all cheer. Everyone seems to be on Lauren's side, like media is the big bad brainwasher. *So stop watching TV and reading the newspaper! What is wrong with you!* I think. As for me, I'll keep turning the pages of my magazines and becoming a better person for it. I can even picture my own face staring back at me from a colour spread.

When the bell rings I leave the class slowly, not wanting to be part of the masses. They're all annoying, as far as I'm concerned. And I drift to my locker. From the corner of my eye I spot Jay chatting in the hall with Lauren. I don't even look their way as I stride past, but he chases after me.

"Hey, wait up, Babe! Isn't it more fun to be a

blonde?" I ignore him and walk more quickly.

"What's a matter, Kimmm?"

I toss my hair back as I round the corner of the hall, still not giving Jay even so much as a glance.

"Slow down, Babe, c'mon!" Jay's so pathetic when he begs.

We step into the cafeteria, where I finally stop and turn towards him. "She's not your type, Jay, honestly."

"Hey, you know you're my only girl." He leans over and tries to kiss me but I push his face away.

He catches one of my hands and holds it, looking straight into my eyes, his head tilted like a sad puppy. Just as I'm about to scratch his head and forgive him, his eyes break away. I check where he's looking.

It's Andrea walking by — or maybe floating's a better word. Besides being thin now, she looks like a ghost. Pale, big faded blue eyes that pop out of her bony face. How does a person go from one extreme — class fatso brainer — to the other: swizzle-stick no-light-on mystery woman? She's caught Jay's interest anyway. I elbow him in the chest.

"C'mon, Kimmm, I'm still alive. I can't help it. I'm a guy."

I open my mouth for a quick comeback — but I only think the words. I stop before telling him. He must take it as a sign that he's forgiven.

"Want to go to the mall with me Saturday?" he asks as I'm about to join the line-up for food. "The new Dozers CD is supposed to be in then."

His voice contains just the right note of pleading, but by now I'm in a really bad mood. Everyone always sides with Ms Smarty Overalls Lauren Dreyburgh. Even Jay likes her better than me. Then he has the nerve to watch Andrea while he's supposed to be begging my forgiveness. There's no way I can agree to anything at this moment. And by Saturday I'll be Barbie, the queen of the mall. I won't need some pathetic boy who can't stop ogling other women.

"No, I don't want to go to the mall with you. Why don't you just go with one of the geek girls? You know, Andrea or Lauren!" Then I flip my hair over my shoulder and stride away, pushing my hips forward. I'll show Jay Friessen.

"Maybe I'll just do that," he sputters.

"Fine, then," I throw back as I grab a salad for my tray.

The rest of the day is too boring for words: classes, homework. Julie comes over after school and she reaches for Kimberly Barbie. "So do you think you got the job?" she asks as she swings the doll's arms back at an awful angle. *What is it with her and dolls' arms?*

I want to snatch Barbie away from her, only at that moment I'm keying in the code to pick up our telephone messages so I grate my teeth. C'mon, c'mon, there's got to be something from Detel and Company, or maybe my agent. Instead Ms Smyrnious's voice talks at me.

"Hello, this is Kimberly's teacher, Ms Smyrnious. I wanted to discuss the results of Kimberly's math test with you. Please call me when you get a chance."

I don't listen to the phone number she gives. I fast forward to the end and then key the code to erase.

"Don't! Leave her alone!" I finally snap at Julie, reaching for Barbie. "I just barely got it back on last time."

Julie clicks her tongue. "Come off it, Kim, her arm can go the full three hundred and sixty degrees." She pulls Barbie away and whips her arm around and around.

"Stop it!" I yell and snatch the doll back. "Next you'll be undressing her and drawing moustaches on her." I sit Kimberly Barbie back down, straightening her bandeau bra.

"Well, I can tell someone's not in the mood for company. I'm going home." Julie takes off out of my room.

I know I should go after her and apologize, but let's face it — there's nothing in the world that gets you into a worse mood than someone commenting on your bad mood in the first place.

Well, maybe there's one thing that can get me in a worse mood. My parents somehow both get home early. That's a pain under any kind of circumstances. Only today they planned it so we can all spend more time together as a family. I hate that. They'll talk to me until I let something slip, I know it.

chapter 18

"Ouch!"

Friday after school I'm in the family room, concentrating on the portable phone in my hand just in case Detel still calls, and trying not to let the 'rents get to me. But Mom's yell is hard to ignore. From my spot on the couch I shift just enough to see her coming out of the laundry room holding a bleeding hand.

"That stupid wire dryer handle you rigged up cut my finger!" she rants at Dad.

"Geez, you must have really yanked at it hard for that duct tape to give out. Let me." My dad stands up from sorting mail at his desk across the hall and they head for the bathroom together. "Look, I've already ordered another handle," he goes on, loud enough to drown out the love scene on TV. "I'm sure it will be in any day."

"Three weeks it took, last time. You actually have to pick it up though." Mom says even louder. Clearly she's feeling the same way I do. I hit the volume button on the remote.

But it's no good. My show is over and there's no more shouting anyway. I hit the OFF button and head for the kitchen to make an appearance.

They both come back, Mom's hand bandaged now. Dad starts fixing drinks for them.

"Set the table, honey, will you?" my mother tells me. "Supper will be ready in a few minutes."

"Was there any mail for me?" I ask. I should have gone through it before Dad saw it, in case something came from *Ms Mode*.

"Well, your dividend cheque arrived today," Dad answers. "Grandma Benson's shares sure are paying off nicely."

"Great," I tell him, setting down the dinner plates. Why do I feel just a tiny bit uneasy?

"I'll deposit the cheque on my lunch hour on Monday," Mom offers.

That's why, I think. My heart starts a new hip hop beat of its own. *They're going to find out about the withdrawals. What am I going to do?*

"Only, do you know where the bankbook is? I've been through the desk twice," Mom says as she stirs whatever's in a pot. "I can't see Kimberly's bankbook anywhere."

I'll have to call Elaine Chev and ask for my modelling money right away.

"The bank will give you a new book," my father says, sipping at a glass.

"But I was sure I kept it in the desk. And I just want to be able to dash in and out." Mom lifts a roasting pan from the oven, then grins. "The automatic timer worked. Chicken's ready."

"Good. I'll look for the bankbook after supper," my father offers. "Sometimes things slip in behind that drawer."

What will he do when he can't find it?

"Kimberly, you lightened your hair!" My mother says suddenly as she brings the potatoes over to the table. Dad brings the chicken.

After two days she finally notices? I think back to that quiz, Are Your 'Rents Driving You Crazy?, and shake my head. Yes, yes, they definitely are. "Just a rinse," I toss off as casually as possible. Why sweat the small stuff? I figure, as I grab the salad from the counter. "Julie and I put it in Tuesday night while we were working on that project."

Mom squints. "It's not bad. I wish you would have mentioned it first, though."

"Didn't I? Sorry, Mom." A hair shade, the least of my worries. "This casserole's really great. And it just baked by itself while you were at work?"

"Yes, for once I set the controls and timer correctly." Mom smiles and then yacks about how well things went at the office too. *Blah, blah, blah.* That set the conversation going in another direction really nicely. At least for a while.

"What's new at work with you?" Mom asks Dad.

"You know Greg Watt's son, the one who's studying to be an engineer?" Dad said. "What's his name again?"

"Kyle, yes, that tall good-looking boy."

"Six feet tall. And lots of muscle. I don't know," my father looks at me and winks. "Do girls like that?"

"Whatever, Dad." I stab a potato. "Go on with your story."

"Oh, there's nothing much to tell. It's just that he works as a tutor at the university. If you need help with your algebra or geometry, Kim, he could certainly use the money."

I just roll my eyes. But then my heart does the hip hop again. How long will it take before Ms Smyrnious calls back? And when will she finally figure out that it's easier to reach my parents at the office?

"Which reminds me. The other day, I could have sworn I saw your doppelgänger," Dad says as he bites into a chicken leg.

"Doppelgänger?"

"Yes, a very close lookalike. What an attractive girl, all dressed in pink. Of course, you look much prettier."

My skin feels hot suddenly. *Don't go red, don't go red!* I tell myself. He hasn't clued in, just don't give yourself away.

"There were lots of beautiful girls in the lobby," he goes on. "Wonder if there was a special promotion going on. Detel's always coming up with some crazy idea."

It's all too much for me. It's as if my parents are accidentally stumbling onto everything. I leave most of my food on the plate and slide my chair back. "May I be excused?" I ask as I stand. "I'm really not very hungry.

"A headache coming?" Mom asks, her brow wrinkling up.

"I hope not," I tell her, but as I head for the phone and key in the modelling agency phone number, I'm not really sure at all.

The phone rings and rings and rings. Finally a phone company operator answers in a recorded message. "I'm sorry. The number you have reached is no longer in service."

Must have pressed a wrong number. I try again. Same voice, same message. And again. And again.

When I give up finally, there's no signal to let me know someone else has called while I was on the phone. Just in case, though, I key in the codes. The same snotty recorded operator voice comes on. "You have *no* new messages in your mailbox." I swear into the receiver and then slam it down.

Maybe Detel will call later, I think, as I gently tug out the last pages of my bankbook. Or maybe the Detel guys changed their mind about the promotion at the mall tomorrow and they'll call another day. That has to be it, I tell myself as I slip downstairs and slide open the drawer on my father's desk to jam the bankbook at the back.

Inspiration hits and I tear up the last pages so the numbers won't be easy to see. They'll never pick up the bits to check the balance — they'll just throw them all out and ask the bank for another bankbook. It looks as though the pages tore out by accident.

Yes, that's what they'll do. And tomorrow's Saturday so I can visit the agency in person to ask for my money. Then I can swing around to the bank to redeposit it and check out the mall, just in case some other Barbie got the job. Though that's really not a possibility, I'm sure of it.

Things will work out. It looked a little dicey there for a bit, but now I know I'm back in control again.

chapter 19

"I'm really sorry about the other day, Julie. It seems like everything is caving in on me." Friendship with Julie means always saying sorry, it seems. But on the other end of the line, Julie seems pretty understanding — something you can't always count on with her — so I continue explaining about what happened with my parents and the bankbook and now I have to get some money in that account fast.

"You only wore the outfit for a few hours. I'm sure you can return everything and get your money back," Julie suggests.

"The shoes too, you think? With those cute little butterflies?" I sigh into the telephone receiver.

"Well, I don't know. How worn do they look? You didn't walk over any gravel or anything. What about the cab fare?"

I take a another deep breath and let it out as a sigh. "I'm hoping they don't remember the exact balance in the bankbook. Since I updated after each withdrawal, when they ask for a new one the first page should just show a new total."

"Hey, you're really smart, Kimberly. I would

have never thought of that."

I smile into the receiver. School marks just don't measure real brain power.

"Meet you at the bus stop in half an hour."

"You got it."

It's a long bus ride to the agency, and when we get there the door's locked.

"I guess she doesn't work on Saturdays," Julie says. "Too bad."

But there's a white sheet of paper tacked up on the inside of the glass.

"What does this mean?" I ask even as I'm reading it. " 'Notice to Renter,' it says at the top . . . then it talks about 'failure to meet payment schedules' and stuff."

"It sounds like Elaine Chev's been locked out of her place. Or maybe she even skipped town or something."

"What about my money! And my professional photo shots?" I pound a fist on the agency door and then kick it, just for something to do. Really, I know the answers to my own questions.

I'm screwed.

I feel so betrayed. After all, if you can't count on an agency that represents such greats as Jan Johannsen and Lianne Ulan, is there anyone out there you can trust?

The agency visit turned out to be such a short

stop, at least we get to use our bus transfer, saving a couple of bucks. But what difference will that make? I think, as the bus pulls up. Even if I can return all my outfits and the shoes, I'll still be over a couple hundred dollars short. There's no way my parents won't pick that up right away.

The bus sways, stops, starts. It's so annoying. I suddenly remember a magazine spread where Lianne Ulan sat in the back of a white stretch limo. If I were Barbie or the *Ms Mode* model of the year, I would always take a limo, and the chauffeur would have to drive smooth or I would fire him. Then it hits me. Maybe that picture of Lianne was just another pose, kind of like the shot of me sitting on that Harley in Gunther's studio. It's not like I ever use a motorcycle for transportation. It's all a big lie.

We get off at the mall and tackle the shoe store first. A young guy serves us and he seems pretty okay about returning our money. MARCUS, his name tag reads, and underneath: SALES ASSOCIATE. He's cute and really earnest, wearing a white shirt that's buttoned right to the top and tucked into belted beige pants.

But then he can't seem to do the paperwork involved. Every time he punches something into the register he frowns. Finally he needs to go into the back and get the manager.

She's pretty young too, so I'm hoping there still

won't be any hassle. But first she eyeballs her sales associate sidekick, then she stares at us. Frowning, she turns the shoes around and around. "These shoes have been worn."

"Of course," I answer. "I tried them on in the store — "

"The bottom is scuffed. We have carpet in here." She places the shoes top down so we can see the scuffing.

"Yes, but it was only after wearing them a bit that I realized they squeezed my feet. And you can't see it at all, but there's a tiny nail head coming through the sole. I got a blister from that." I out-stare Miss Manager just barely.

"We can repair them or exchange them. We can't give you back your money," she tells us, folding her arms across her chest.

"But there's nothing else we like," Julie pipes in.

"Take a credit, then," Miss Manager shoots back.

"Oh, come on." I grab the shoes and shove them back into the bag. "I'm never going to buy from this store again," I say as I toss my hair back.

But it is one of my favourite shoe stores. The next time I need shoes, I'll just have to make sure only Marcus is working.

We head for the Patches Boutique next. I'm not feeling really confident about anything anymore. Nothing's going my way. But I try to keep my shoulders back, my hips forward — no one will know by my walk. I stride with long steps. Then I see something that sucks out all my breath for a full minute at least. I'm sure my heart stops too.

"Welcome, Barbie!" the banner over the stage reads. There's a pink throne in the middle and a display of doll houses, furniture, clothing and other accessories.

Honk, honk! A horn blasts at us from the other direction. We turn to see a pink convertible driving towards us. A crowd of little kids and their parents follow alongside.

I want to throw up. It should be me sitting in that car, waving, smiling. I'm the true Barbie in this mall. Only the person who waves back to the kids is Nina.

The convertible stops. A really cute tall Asian guy steps from the crowd. He's wearing tails and a top hat and he's young. Don't tell me, it can't be!

He helps Nina from the car and I guess that makes it official. He's Ken.

"Well that really sucks," Julie says.

I squeeze my eyes tight for a moment. "Yes, it does."

A line of little girls has already formed, all anxious to meet and talk with her in person.

I shove through them. "Excuse me, excuse me. Sorry. Barbie's my friend. I need to talk to her just for a second," I tell the girl at the head of the line. *"Psst,* Nina! I don't believe it. Congratulations."

She gives me such a great smile, I can tell she thinks I mean it. She bends towards me, cupping a hand around her mouth so no one else will hear. "I'm sorry you didn't get it, honey. But I need this. It's steady work and I've got a little girl of my own to look after at home."

I pull back, shocked. Nina looks so young, eighteen, max.

The first kid in line scampers up and there's a photographer snapping their pictures.

I stare. It could have been *me*. For a moment I feel like telling the photographer and everyone, She's a phony! Barbie's not a single mother!

But then the next kid runs up, climbs up on Nina's lap to touch her tiara. And then I decide Barbie's come a long way. Why not? For today at least, Barbie is too a single mother.

I back away and wave.

"What do you want to do?" Julie says.

I sigh. "Let's get rid of the pink. I'm never going to wear that colour again."

We walk over to the Patches Boutique, which happens to be across from the Economart. This time SUMMER, Manager, serves us.

"I'm sorry," I explain. "In this store light, I thought the pink really looked good on me. But when I stepped outside, I knew I could never be happy in it."

"Oh yeah, this is definitely not your shade. If I'd

been serving you, I would never have let you leave the store with it."

Thank you, Summer.

"Do you have your receipt?" She takes the skirt and top from me.

"Yes, right here." I pass her the bill from the bag. "And here are the tags."

"Great. You're making my job easy." She scans the code on the tags and makes me sign a return note. "Here you go!" She hands me my money. "Come back soon."

"Now *that's* service," Julie says.

I'm pretty happy about at least that one thing today, until Julie suddenly freezes. "Uh-oh!"

"What? What's wrong?" I look to where she's pointing, since she won't just tell me.

And there's Jay walking with his arm around Lauren.

I freeze for a second too, then I turn and grab Julie's elbow. "Hurry, hurry. I want to get out of here. This is the most embarrassing moment of my life."

chapter 20

Sunday I'm so depressed, I don't even want to get out of bed. I reach for one of Julie's magazines on my night table and it flops down to the floor. I pick it up and what a coincidence — it's opened up to a quiz. I guess the quiz pages are right dead centre where the staples are, so it's not a big surprise.

I frown as I read the quiz title: Is Your Boytoy Worthy? Another amazing coincidence? Maybe. Only — let's face it — they have that same quiz in every other magazine issue, just worded differently. I almost let the magazine drop, because really, I already know the answer. Jay fits into the lowest category: Toenail Sludge.

Something makes me pull it back up to my bed. Besides being depressed, I'm really bored. So I read the questions. Maybe knowing all the answers will make me feel better about everything.

> It's your birthday and your passionate puppy forgot, so he:
>
> (a) runs out at lunch and buys you some roses.
> (b) draws up some coupons, good for your choice of date, movie and dinner.

(c) hides on you at school and fakes a cold when he calls you later.

Honestly, these choices aren't even realistic. How could anyone hide at school? And drawing coupons, that's something I used to do when I forgot Mother's Day. Who would do that for their girlfriend? I know that Jay will score well for (a) — even though he would never dream of paying for the roses.

> Your family hosts a dinner and you invite your sugar puff. He:
>
> (a) never shows — says he can't handle the family thing, what with his parents being split up and all.
> (b) refuses to make small talk or join in the charades game — basically sulks because he wants you all to himself.
> (c) calls your dad Sir, shakes his hand, compliments your mom on everything from her outfit to the napkins on the table. He knows how to fit in and does.

Okay, he's scoring really well on this one. He's definitely (c). Last time he came over, he talked computers with Dad till I wanted to hurl. He ate two plates of Mom's roast beef, which I thought was entirely too fatty. Plus he brought flowers he'd picked from his own garden, not the florist's.

> You have to get braces, and when you tell your boytoy, he:

(a) kisses you long and slow, then wonders out loud how it will feel when your teeth are covered in steel.

(b) shrugs his shoulders. It's no biggie, your lips are what's important, not your teeth.

(c) suggests you see other people, that you're both too young to be tied down.

I decide Jay would be a (b) for this one so he's still racking up points in the worthiness department.

You flunk algebra and the 'rents insist on summer school. Your cutie:

(a) has a summer job anyways, so you'll meet later after homework's done.

(b) promises to walk you to school and to be waiting when you're finished.

(c) sympathizes with you but starts scoping for your replacement immediately.

Flunking math . . . summer school . . . Oh my gawd, I never thought of that. I chew at two fingernails at the same time. Is there still time to improve? I can't spend my summer in that hot smelly school. I take a breath to calm down. Think . . . Think . . . What would Jay do? I remember how he came with me to the photography shoot, how Gunther barred him from the studio and how Jay waited, bought me a drink and then kissed me. He'd wait for me at summer school. I know it. Only problem is, he'd scope girls while I was in class, when I was out, and while I was with him.

Your best friend doesn't have a date and wants to go with you and your guy to the show. He:

(a) tells you no way, you never get enough time alone as it is.
(b) gallantly buys her popcorn too. A friend of yours is his friend too.
(c) starts flirting like crazy with her.

Well, Jay's not crass enough to flirt with Julie. He'd even swipe her a candy bar too. But it's what he does behind my back with people who aren't my friends that really bothers me. There's a bunch more questions, but none of them are the right ones to get at the bad things about him. Jay ends up in the top category: Perfect Love Dove:

You can take him anywhere and he's kind and considerate. He truly wants to make you happy and thinks of you first.

What do they know? I think and fling the magazine across the room. So much for the quiz making me feel better. And I hardly needed to have to worry about summer school. Aaargh!

I guess if I knew the answers I really needed, I would feel great. Like what am I going to do about the missing money in my account. I rake my hair up with my fingers, fluffing it back. Unfortunately, the one person who might know is my Toenail Sludge Love Dove, and I'm not talking to him. I can't help sighing. No matter what, I miss him.

I decide to clean my room. Putting things in order helps me feel more in control sometimes. Still in my boxers and T-shirt, I haul out the vacuum cleaner and let it rip. I push the wand into every corner. I attack the heating duct, slide the brush over every slat of my blinds, down the folds of my balloon drapes. Then I move my Barbies and vacuum the shelves. Nina can't be a real Barbie, what do those Detel people know? She can be a Barbie friend, sure! Multiculturalism is a big thing in our neighbourhood, I know. But to represent Barbie! I mean, I had to take a big fashion risk to colour my hair.

I position the girls back in their places. Single-mother Barbie, hmph. Everyone knows Barbie is strictly Big Sister material. I saw a Basketball Player Barbie the other day. She wore kneepads and a sweatband along with her uniform. Imagine Barbie sweating.

I'm sweating by the time I finish my room, and it's not all because of my cleaning aerobics. I've done a little mental review. I didn't get the Barbie job, and Chevron's gone under. There's no way I can replace all the money I've taken from my account. I'm going to get caught. While I take my shower, I think I might as well forget about it and just take whatever comes.

chapter 21

Monday morning, everything looks dull and grey — my mother's outfit, the wires sticking out where the dryer handle is supposed to be, the sky as we drive to school, my life. With no Barbie job or Chevron agency, the only thing left in my modelling future is the *Ms Mode* search, and I haven't even heard from them. Which leaves me with what kind of chance with them?

Zero, probably.

And no Jay either, to pump some excitement bubbles into me. Ms Smyrnious's voice drones on, like the hum of a dull grey bug. I look over at Jay in his seat. He takes me for granted, obviously. I think back to that article, 31 Ways to Make Your Hottie Pant, and realize I haven't been following their advice. I should probably try to make Jay jealous around now. I turn away from him and try to listen to Ms Smyrnious.

Just a little over a month of school left, I tell myself. Hang in there. But then yesterday's quiz comes back to me. Not the part about Jay being a Love Dove, but the idea of summer school. Ugh! The threat hits me with such a *whomp*. I know I have to do something about that now. And just like that, the answer comes to me — killing two birds with one stone! When Ms Smyrnious stops droning I raise my hand and she calls on me.

"Ms Smyrnious, about your phone call to my parents. My father has already found a tutor for me. He's in university." I smile as I tell her. How can I not smile: six feet tall, lots of muscles . . . If that tutor doesn't make my hottie pant too, I'll give up taking quizzes for life.

"Well, that's good news, Kim. Perhaps I could run off some material for you to give to him."

"Um, yes, that will be a big help." She bought it! That's great. No discussion with my parents, no finding out about forged signatures on tests or absentee notes. My smile stretches even wider.

In language arts we get our last project for the year, creating an issue of our own magazine.

"I want at least one research article, a cover story and a question-and-answer column," Ms Smyrnious tells us. "Of course, I need to know your target market, and you should have at least three ads and a table of contents."

Yesss, finally something I can really sink my teeth into. Imagine the research, buying every magazine on the stand, all in the name of homework. I can write all kinds of embarrassing moments. I can do make-up tips. I can even do a real-life makeover and put the before and after shots in the magazine. An A on a project! Maybe that will help my average on my report card and get me out of summer school.

The day starts turning a shade brighter. Not pink exactly — I still have the missing money and my parents to deal with, after all.

In family studies I tackle the toughest part of the dress I'm sewing, the zipper — at least that's what Ms Ferris tells me. She makes me check with her on each step, when really it's all a matter of common sense and following instructions. Place, pin and stitch. The zipper slides up and down easily when I'm done, the tiny flap of material over it lies down smoothly, the stitching around it is straight and even.

"Excellent! At this rate you'll be finished before the end of the week," Ms Ferris says. "Go ahead and work on the straps next."

By lunch bell I'm double-stitching the ends of the straps to the dress, and wondering whether with my new hair colour the dress would also look good on me in some shade of green, mint or even emerald.

The dress almost makes me forget the other problem I have to face. Which is, of course, the humiliation of Jay cheating on me with Lauren. And there she is in the lunchtime line-up. Guess I have to deal with that problem now. Luckily sewing clears my mind and helps me relax. I smile. I'm not going to give Lauren Dreyburgh the satisfaction of thinking she stole my boyfriend. I'm going to pretend that Jay and I were never together, that I'm pleased for her. That will make her wonder, and it will sure confuse the heck out of my love cookie.

Instead of lining up, I cut in ahead of her.

She has the nerve to give me a dirty look. Well, I'm above all that. So I compliment her on her new jeans, tell her how slim she looks in them. "Told you he'd think you were cute if you lost weight."

But — get this — she's ticked with me. "Jay never said anything like that."

"Well, not in so many words, he's a guy. They don't analyze stuff, they just react. He took you out, didn't he?"

"You're such a liar, Kimberly."

Excuse me! She's sniping at me like I've humiliated her in front of the whole world, instead of vice versa. That's what I get for trying to be nice to her. I flip my hair back and try to ignore her as I buy my lunch. But Lauren follows me back to my table.

Now she blasts Jay. Says something like, "You either return the CD you stashed in my backpack, or I will. And I'll tell the manager who stole it."

I'm cluing in finally. Lauren thinks I had something to do with planning a shoplift with Jay, one that could have gotten her in trouble. Now she's going to turn Jay in.

Jay doesn't look really good. His face pales, but in splotches, so that he looks like he has two white dots on his cheek. "The manager's never going to believe you," he sputters.

"Oh no? My sister works there and the manager knows me." She stomps off.

Jay turns my way now and says, "I never liked her for one minute, you gotta know that. I only went to the mall with her because you wouldn't."

"Would you have stashed the CD in *my* bag then?" I can't resist asking.

"Never. Come on. It was only a game because I knew her sister worked security. I let her see me pick up the Dozers CD so she would try to catch me. You have to believe me."

And part of me does. I mean, I know he's not really the perfect Love Dove, but he's not absolute Toenail Sludge either. Still, seeing his arm around Lauren hurt. I just can't jump into forgiving him so easily. "That's okay," I tell him. "I think we both should see other people. I've been meaning to tell you. There's this guy I'm planning on going out with. He's in university . . . "

An amazing thing happens when you just relax. The solutions to your problems just land flat in your lap.

I turn down Julie's lift in the mom-mobile after school — I'm in no big hurry to get home and have to explain my bankbook to my own mother. So I drift slowly up and down sidewalks. The sky's still dull and grey, and step by slow step I still end up where I don't want to be.

Just as I head up our walkway, though, the clouds start breaking apart and a little bit of sun peeks through. It's like a sign.

Mom's car's in the driveway. "Hello?" I call as I open the door, waiting for the yelling to start.

Nothing.

Her briefcase sits in the middle of the hall. Her shoes lie sprawled around it. Not like her. She puts everything away immediately. I knock on the bathroom door, but it just opens as my knuckles hit it. No one in there.

Nobody in the kitchen or the family room. I check Dad's office and spot his pile of mail on the left corner of the desk. One bright-coloured postcard sticks out among the opened window envelopes. It's from *Ms Mode*. Dad's not home yet. So it all has to be Friday's mail.

Why didn't he tell me! He hates my magazines, that's why. Probably didn't look past the address.

I flip the card over, my hands shaking. Could this be it? Little bubbles pop in my stomach.

Dear Kimberly Rainer:

You are invited to an interview Monday, June 2, at 5:30 P.M. at the Harbourlight Hotel.

Good luck in the Great Model Search!

Sincerely,

Francesca Livingston, Editor

Yesss! Who cares about Barbie? This is another good sign, I know it. Just one week to decide what to wear and how to do my hair. Will there be enough time after school to change and put fresh make-up on? A million questions float up in pink bubbles inside me, making me forget my first one for a moment.

Where's Mom?

The lights are all off everywhere too. A clue. I head for her bedroom and tap gently on the door. I hear a soft moan so I push it open.

She's lying on the bed, still in her grey suit, with a cloth on her forehead and her eyes closed.

"Is it bad?" I ask. I know without asking she's got a migraine. Hey, it runs in the family.

"Mmmhmmm," she answers in another moan.

"Do you want me to get you one of your pills, Mom?"

"No, I took three already."

I hesitate, then, "Um, you didn't deposit Grandma's cheque, did you?" I ask.

"No, Kim. My head . . . it started right after coffee break."

"That's okay." I really feel bad for her, honestly I do. Which makes me offer to make supper. And one other thing . . . " You know, Mom, I'm at the mall all the time. There's no reason I can't deposit my own money. Save you the trip." Well, it's true, I can — along with the money I got back for returning

182

my Barbie outfit. My parents really don't need to know everything right now. Once I get the *Ms Mode* job, nothing I did will look so bad.

chapter 22

"This tuna casserole is delicious," Dad tells me.
"It's so nice of you to cook supper. We could have
gone out, you know."

"No problem," I tell him. Cat food, really. I mean,
two tins of fish, some macaroni. But like everything, it's all in the presentation. I added some
chopped red peppers, a generous handful of fresh
mushrooms.

"The sauce is lovely."

And a tin of mushroom soup. "Thank you. Um,
Dad, I think I need the math tutor."

"Kyle Watts, you mean?" Dad looks up from his
noodles for a minute.

"Is that his name?" I ask innocently.

Dad nods. "I'll arrange something right after
supper." He has another forkful of catfood. "Don't
worry, honey. Everyone needs a little help now and
again." And another forkful. "How are your other
courses going?"

"Good, good. Which reminds me. I have this
media project where I have to research lots of magazines. Could you give me some money to buy
some?"

He pulls out his wallet and opens it. "How much? Ten do it?"

I scrunch my mouth. "Twenty might if Julie and I share. And by the way, I'm going to work at her house after school tomorrow. I probably won't be home for supper."

"Here you go," Dad says and pushes a bill over to me.

I suddenly remember an answer from that quiz, Are You Getting What You Want Out of Life? I think it was (c). Something to do with inventing lots of field trips and friends' birthdays to get extra money. If you did it in lots of small doses, your 'rents wouldn't notice. Maybe that's how I could get at least part of the photo shoot money back to my account!

I also remember my category: Surfer. I smile. Maybe I should take the quiz over again. I think by now I could have really become a Steamroller.

When I call Julie she seems as excited as I am over the postcard from *Ms Mode*, even offers to come with me to the appointment. Sometimes she really can be a good friend — if I keep her away from breakables. And if she can tear herself away from her yearbookies. We talk a bit about what I'm going to wear. Not pink, that's for sure. I'm feeling really mellow so I compliment Julie. "Just think, it was all because of your picture taking. I think you're on your way."

"I think so too," she answers. "See you tomorrow, then."

With the close call about the bank account, I don't dare buy a new outfit for the *Ms Mode* appointment. Instead I try on all my and Julie's clothes over the next week, and decide the night before that my blue dress has served me well. So I run a quick hand-wash cycle in the washing machine to freshen it, pull the stupid wire handle to put it in the dryer, and pull the dress out the minute the buzzer goes off, so that it doesn't have any wrinkles.

I hang it up and choose all my accessories to go with it too. A blue floating stone necklace, some matching earrings. For the shoes, hmm. A stroke of brilliance — I take out my white pair, the ones I couldn't return, and with nail polish turn the little butterflies blue.

It should have hit me yesterday while I was getting everything ready. There was another big problem that I was totally ignoring. How could I not see it?

At least I should have thought of it this morning as I was designing the three advertisements for my magazine project in language arts. Or for sure in family studies when I was stitching the hem on my little black dress. All week long it was sitting there right in front of me. But my mind was full of other things. The square slits on either side of the dress turned out really well, sort of an exotic oriental touch. I almost wanted to wear it for the interview this afternoon, if only I had time to accessorize it.

I guess the problem was such a part of me I couldn't see it. Julie finally brought it up at the end of lunch break.

"What are you planning to do about your nails, Kim? I thought you were using Bite-stop."

My nails . . . Oh my gosh, she's right! It was something Elaine Chev had noticed and warned me about. I'd chewed down my nails to the quick. Well, the last few days were so stressful. Now the skin around my nails looks red, which might really attract the *Ms Mode* interviewer's eyes. "I *am* using Bite-stop. I've just acquired a taste for it."

Julie shakes her head like she's looking at a bad accident at the side of the road.

"Don't do that!" I grab her. "You have to help me! This is my big chance!"

She looks thoughtful for a moment. "What about acrylic nails? Ms Chev's French manicure probably wasn't real either."

"Yes, you're right! Only don't I need an appointment with a nail expert for that?" I bend my hands into fists now so that my nails are hidden. How could I have done this to myself!

"For a really good set, yes. But this is an emergency. We'll just get some stick-ons." Julie gets up and puts her lunch wrappers in the garbage.

"What time is your appointment again?"

"Five-thirty."

"That doesn't leave us a lot of time. Barely four hours." She taps her chin with a finger and I notice for the first time her nails are perfect. They're filed into a lovely shape and coated in a robin's egg blue. If I hadn't chewed mine down, I could have borrowed her polish. It would have gone perfectly with what I'm planning to wear.

"Tell you what. Go home and get ready for your appointment. Then we'll meet at Economart and buy the nails there. We can always stick them over your nails while we're riding on the bus if we're really running late."

"Oh, I'm so glad you're my friend. What would I do without you?" I can't believe that — just like Jay did for the photo shoot — Julie is planning to come with me. Couldn't be much fun for her to watch *me* go for glory.

My last class is gym again, but we're doing a unit on dance so there's no outdoor escape. You think that dance could be really interesting, but we're learning line dancing, and even if that wasn't something my grandmother did in her spare time, my mind wants to deal with the problem at hand. I miss all the stupid little side steps because I'm worried about my nails!

Finally the bell rings and I take off, still wearing my gym things, leaving my street clothes in my locker. I chase after a bus that's just pulled away and actually get the driver to stop. That's a very good sign.

At home I jump into the shower and perform the world's quickest hair wash. Still it's four by the time I'm out. The doorbell rings a bunch of times as I'm towelling dry. *Wash and wear hair, just like Mom.* I wince.

Who could it be? I wonder as I shimmy into a slip, but then decide I just don't have time for whoever it is. No time for a sales or religion pitch, no time to hunt for change for the paper girl. Ugh, dressing while I'm still damp and in a hurry's really getting to be a bad habit. Well, I don't have any time for myself . . . I hear my mother's words again, the ones she said after I commented on her hit-and-miss make-up job. Am getting to be like her, not taking enough time to look good?

Gently, gently, the pantyhose roll up. I manage to pull them on without snags. Well, of course it's because I have no nails.

Necklace and earrings go on, blue mascara — what a great touch — a bit of that Barbie frosted lipstick. I'd have liked to do concealer and foundation, with shading around my brows, but there's simply no time. Still I take a moment to look in the full-length mirror. Front . . . back . . . over my shoulder . . . Perfect. Nah, I'm safe. I don't look a bit like Mom.

My hair's still wet, but as it dries it forms little curls. I help them along with my fingers as I rush to collect my bag.

I'm ready!

As I head out the door I spot something that melts my heart. There's a bunch of red roses hanging from the mailbox. Guess who they're from? I read his card.

> You are the only one for me. Good luck,
> Jay

Awww! He always knows how to cheer me up at the right moment. Now I have to go back into the house and put them in a vase. I don't take the time to trim the ends or throw the envelope of Stay-alive in the water. I set them on my desk, rush out again and slam the door behind me.

I chase down another bus and the driver stops again. This is a record. My luck is really holding out. It's four forty-five when I get to the mall.

Julie's waiting at the fountain for me and we head for the make-up aisles of Economart. It's a little slow getting around the crowds of older people there today. I can't believe all the shoppers. "What gives, Julie? Is it a special sale?"

"First Monday of the month," Lauren Dreyburgh answers from out of nowhere. "Seniors' Day. I know because my grandmother's here buying all our paper towels and soap at fifteen percent off."

"Bully," I mutter. There's no time to chat her up and find out if she's really going to blow the whistle on Jay about the stolen CD. Instead we lose Lauren as we dash around another group of silver-haired women eyeing athletic footwear.

"Which ones?" I ask Julie when we finally find the false nails hanging in little plastic bags from a steel hook in a display.

"These," Julie says and she grabs some. "No time to think."

I tear off after her to the cash. This is where my luck runs out. There's a long snake of older people in front of every cash. They all seem to have a wagon-load of toiletries too.

I close my eyes. *Now* what?

Julie rips open the bag. "Start sticking!" she tells me.

Each nail comes with a little two sided gluey tab. But I have to pull off the plastic cover before they stick. And it's really hard to do that with no nails. Julie helps me.

What a miracle. As each nail sticks on, my hands start to take on a glamour of their own. If only I could have painted them blue too. The last one goes on, but we're still four older people away from the cash. The lady at the head has a bunch of coupons and the cashier is reading the small print on one of them and shaking her head.

Five-fifteen.

"We can't wait any longer. What are we going to do?" Julie panics now.

I take a deep breath. There are so many people around today. I look to the left and then to the right. I wonder where Patricia, Lauren's sister, is.

Nowhere.

It can all end here, I think. I can wait and wait and finally pay and show up a half an hour late when the *Ms Mode* interviewers are folding away their papers into their briefcases. They'll shake their heads. Ms Mode must meet her appointments after all. I can come that close and lose it all. My world can stay dull and grey just like my parents'.

Or — I look around again, bubbles forming and rising inside of me — I can take this one chance. I'm on a roll . . . I'm a winner . . . Nothing's going to spoil this day for me. I take a deep breath and smile. "Go on outside Julie, I'll meet you."

Julie smiles back. She knows exactly what I'm planning. "See you soon."

One more look around. I'm on the roller coaster now, screaming inside as I dodge an older gentleman browsing through the cough drops.

A shopping cart bumps into my hip and I nearly jump out of my skin. "Sorry, dear." It's a lady with a wagon full of Snack-o-Jacks — Economart's own combination of caramel popcorn and chocolate covered nuts. She must have twenty boxes of them.

Geez, how much can she eat? Won't they ruin her dentures?

"That's all right, don't mention it," I tell her. She has unusually bouncy silver hair, and her skin looks really smooth for her age. I smile, then I stride towards the space beside the cash registers. I'm almost there. The bubbles pop inside me. I feel so alive. I'm passing through. There's no one around me anywhere. I'm outside and I'm free! I've done it! Now I can be on time for my interview.

I see Julie in the distance and wave. She starts to lift her arm and then drops it quickly. There's a strange look on her face. She shakes her head and backs up. "What's wrong with you?" I ask, but instead of answering she turns and runs away.

Suddenly I feel a tap on my shoulder and spin around.

It's a tall dark-haired woman with a swollen red nose. She's wearing a grey-blue uniform and on the sleeve there's a label reading GOLDWALL SECURITY.

chapter 23

"That's the one!" The old lady with the bouncy grey hair and Snack-o-Jacks points to me from the entrance of Economart. "She stuck the nails on and walked out without paying."

The security guard asks me to step over to the information desk. Then she makes me empty my bag.

The roller coaster inside me barrels down, a million miles a second. I can feel everything inside me racing out of control as the woman with the swollen nose picks out the empty false nail package.

"But I *wanted* to pay! It's only that the line was too long."

The security guard looks over to the older woman. "What do you think, Jasmine?"

She shakes her head. "That young fella that just bonked you on the beak?"

"Yeah?" The woman fingers the bridge of her nose and sniffs gingerly.

"This one's always hanging around with him." She shakes her head a second time.

Jay? Jay hit *a security guard?*

The tall woman grabs my elbow and starts tugging me towards the back of the store.

"Can I explain this to someone?" I pull my elbow away. "Is Patricia Dreyburgh around?" Lauren's sister would understand. I mean, she was so nice to me in kindergarten.

"She's in the hospital. Got jumped by a drunk Saturday. Hasn't been a good month for Security." The dark-haired lady talks in a really nasal tone. "Why don't you explain it to me?"

"Listen," I force myself to speak softly and calmly. "I have this really important interview for an international fashion magazine in less than fifteen minutes. Can I just pay you?"

"You should have done that in the first place," Snack-o-Jacks-Jasmine pipes in. "You kids think the whole world revolves around you."

"But it's not my fault!" My voice goes high on me. I can't control it. "If there had been an express checkout, none of this would have happened. I mean, I was sticking the nails on in line because I didn't have any time!"

"Nothing's ever their fault," Jasmine grumbles.

The security guard frowns. "You better come with me. No trouble now, mind." She picks up my elbow again.

Neither of them seems to be listening to me.

The older shoppers are parting for the three of us — not like they could do that for me before, when I was in a hurry. Noooo, then they were too weak and arthritic, too busy checking prices. But now they have nothing to do so they're staring at me. "Can you just let go of my arm and slow down. You're making a scene."

The security guard grunts but her grip doesn't loosen.

Now I see someone else staring at me from the shoe department. It's Emily Urbaniak from our school, and she's with a couple of Julie's yearbook workies. They all stare too. Emily's mouth turns down. She feels sorry for me. I straighten my shoulders. The other workies look like they're fighting to keep a straight face. One is smirking, the other's eyebrows are touching her hair.

I'm going to be the school headlines this month. I close my eyes for a second and swallow a ragged breath. I can't cry in front of them, it will only make things worse, so I breathe in again slowly, open my eyes and pick up the pace. The faster we get out of sight the better.

We go through the swinging EMPLOYEES ONLY doors and step into an office. On the wall hangs a bulletin board with about ten Polaroid photographs. One of them looks to be a fresh one of Jay.

In the centre of the room there's a grey modular desk unit with a computer, telephone and a small digital clock on it. The digits read 5:20. In ten minutes my big chance at a real modelling career will take place. Only I won't be there. A knot forms at the bottom of my throat. I can't swallow.

The security guard pulls a chair to the side of the desk for me to sit down. Jasmine plunks herself down on another at the front of the desk. For an old lady, she's pretty casual.

I notice the part in her hair is weird too, tight with no scalp showing, like the hair's woven together. That's it. Jasmine must be wearing a wig. As her fingers drumroll on the desk I see that her hands are smooth and she's wearing a school ring. The security shopper isn't a senior citizen after all. That's just her disguise.

The guard sits down and keys something into her computer. "Name?" she asks as she pauses.

"Can't you just let me go this once?" I look up at her. If only I can get her to let me off, maybe this will still turn out all right. "I've never done anything like this before. Please?"

She's staring at me, fingers hunching over the keyboard. For a moment I can actually feel my hopes rising, like everything inside me is lifting and reaching higher and higher, the way a roller coaster climbs to the top of the loop. Then it hovers for just a second. I stop breathing as I wait.

Just then Jasmine kind of snuffles into a hand, interrupting. "I'm going to get myself something to eat." She stands up, grinning. "Want some more ice for that nose?"

197

Oh, perfect. Now the guard remembers about Jay. The moment is over, I can tell. The roller coaster crashes downward.

"No," the security guard calls back. Jasmine leaves the room. "No," she says to me too. "Your friend tried to make off with a portable CD player not ten minutes ago."

There are no more chances now, even though I keep trying — begging actually. "But I wasn't with him," I whisper.

"Today, you weren't," she answers, with her fingers still ready. "Would you kindly remove the store property from your hands."

I stare down at my hands and start picking off the nails.

"Name?" she repeats.

"Kimberly Rainer." I mumble into my fingers.

"Address and phone number?"

I answer again as she picks up the phone and presses the numbers.

"You're not calling my parents, are you?"

She nods.

"Oh, please don't. Please!"

But it's all too late. Someone at home picks up. *Let it be Mom, come on, come on.* "Good afternoon. Mr. Rainer? This is Goldwall Security from Economart in Fairview Mall."

Dad is going to kill me.

"I'm sorry to have to tell you this, but we just

caught your daughter shoplifting." There's a big pause on the other line. "That's right. Would you kindly come down and pick her up. Ask at the courtesy desk and they'll direct you. Thank you."

Jasmine returns to the room now, chewing, with a sandwich in her hand. The guard pulls a Polaroid camera from the desk and asks me to look towards the lens.

"Why are you taking my picture?" My voice is breaking now.

"You won't be allowed in this store again for a year," Jasmine answers, pointing over to the bulletin board. "That's our record."

Banned from Economart — I face the camera and the light flashes — this is the most humiliating moment of my life. My insides start to ache. It's hard to breathe or swallow. It would be better if I could die before Dad gets here. I rip off the rest of the stick-ons, leaving them in a disgusting looking pile near the digital clock.

The numbers now read 5:30. I shut my eyes against the burning, but I still feel tears leaking down my cheeks. My last chance at modelling is over now too. My life is finished.

chapter 24

Even though I know he's ready to kill me, my father looks all business when he arrives at the security office. He's wearing a grey suit paired with a navy blue pinstriped shirt and a mauve silk tie. The tie was a Father's Day present from me, and I take that as a good sign. He wouldn't wear the present of someone he wants to strangle, would he? Dad knows I'm not some kind of juvenile delinquent. He'll be on my side with these two, won't he?

"Good afternoon, Mr. Rainer. I'm so glad you could come down on such short notice," Jasmine says. She pulls up another chair for him and he sits down.

"I didn't think I had a choice."

Jasmine smiles and tells him about how I was caught with the stick-ons. She enjoys her job, it's clear, and talks to him as though he's another teenage-hating adult. Dad answers yes and no and "Oh really," when she tells him about me hanging around with Jay, and how he's just committed assault and is up for charges. His voice is calm, too calm, like something he's forcing.

She finishes by pinning up my picture on the

bulletin board and telling him about how I won't be allowed on the premises for a year.

"But there won't be any charges laid against Kimberly?" Dad asks.

"Not this time," she says. "Let's hope she's learned her lesson."

Dad stands now and motions to me. "We're free to go then?"

The security guard nods.

"Thank you," Dad says.

As we leave the office he turns to me. "Don't say a word. We'll talk about this when we get home. Your mother's waiting."

Through the mall, down to the underground parking, I chase after him. It feels like the knot in my throat has grown into this huge lead ball and sunk down into my chest. When I slide into the front passenger seat, something cardboard brushes against my thigh. It's a brand new bankbook. I pick it up quickly and the roller coaster takes another lower dip. It's a bankbook for my college savings account. Stuffed in the middle are some larger loose pages. I see the string of my withdrawals listed on them.

"Dad, I'm — "

"Not a word," he repeats, one warning finger in the air.

The silence in the car winds me up tighter and tighter. The ball grows larger till I feel I'm going to choke. We pull out of the parking garage. Dad only watches the road, saying nothing, driving smoothly, like we're on our way to a picnic. When we finally roll into the driveway he gets out slowly. Only then he slams the door so hard the little evergreen air freshener tree takes a spin around the mirror.

Inside the house, sitting at the kitchen table with arms folded across his chest, Dad demands that I start talking.

I tackle the bankbook first. "Remember, Mom, when you wouldn't give me the two hundred dollars for that modelling agency thing? Well, I just couldn't let it go, not without trying."

Dad turns to look at Mom. "You *told* her then."

"No, never. Maybe I should have." She turns to me. "Go on."

"But I don't understand what you just — "

"Go on."

"O-okay. So . . . I took the money from my college account."

Dad's shaking his head now.

"Honestly, Mom . . . Dad . . . I'll never go anyway. I'm just not smart enough. But modelling I thought I could do, could be *good* at even. And I thought it would be exciting." I take a deep breath. "I even got a job right away, so I knew I could deposit the money back again. Only the Chevron Agency closed without paying me."

"The modelling business never changes," Dad

says, still shaking his head. "Chevron Agency, eh?" He removes his gold pen from his lapel pocket and jots down the name. "I'll see about chasing down that money."

"You'll do that?" I take a breath and really look at him, all business but with that touch of colour around his neck. He raises one eyebrow and the edges of his mouth curl just a little. If anyone can track Elaine Chev down, my father can. "But I . . . " I'd better spill it all out. "I also took some money to buy an outfit and some hair dye." I tell them about auditioning for Barbie.

"So that *was* you in the Detel building," Dad says. "You looked just like the doll, actually."

I smile at him for half a second.

"But why didn't you just pay for the artificial nails?" my mother interrupts.

Now I explain about the *Ms Mode* audition and biting my nails and Economart. As I talk I feel lower and lower. The lead ball inside me swells and threatens to close up my throat. I can hardly breathe. That horrible, ugly store with that stupid fake-old-lady shopper . . . all the kids and old ladies that saw me, the security guard with the fat nose . . . all of them staring and looking down on me . . . my picture on that bulletin board . . . It's so humiliating. I can't live with it. I can never go back to school again and face anyone.

But there's nothing left for me. Because after all

that work — the picture taking, the entry writing — I missed my appointment for the Great Model Search, my one big chance to escape the grey prison walls of school. I'm sobbing by the time I finish.

My parents act weird, no yelling. Instead Dad reaches across the table and holds Mom's hand. I don't want to see that. I want this all over with, I want to be screamed at and then let off the hook.

When Mom finally tells me I'm grounded for a month, I don't even feel bad about that. I will never leave the house again anyway.

The phone rings three times and my chair at the kitchen table is closest. I can see that it's Julie's number in the display window. I automatically reach for it even though I have nothing to say to her. Traitor. She could have warned —

"No TV or phone either." Dad grabs the receiver instead. "She can't!" he snaps. "And don't call back for a month." He bangs the receiver back on the hook.

"No Julie," Mom says. "No calls. The only people you'll see are the ones in your class while you're at school."

"But I can't go back — "

"You *will* go back to school," Mom continues. "Education is important!"

"But everyone will be laughing at me!" I sob into my arms on the table.

"This will blow over, Kim," my father tells me, stroking my hair. "If you never shoplift again, everyone will forget, believe me. There are other things going on in the world."

The phone rings again, from an unknown number this time.

Dad picks up again. I can hear Julie's voice: "Sorry, wrong number," she says. Then there's a *click*.

Dad slams the phone down. "Maybe we should talk about the company you keep. I don't ever want you to see Jay again."

Dad's words hit my stomach like a fist. No Jay? I can't even breathe, let alone argue. My eyes feel hot and sore from crying, and behind them a pounding starts.

"We'll talk about this again when we're all feeling better." Dad tells me. "In the meantime, your mother and I are going out for supper. There's some tuna casserole in the fridge. Don't answer the phone unless you see it's our cell number."

All of that's fine. I'm not about to eat anything — certainly not cat food — at that moment, and I don't want to talk to anyone, especially not Julie. *No Jay?* I head up to my room and finger the velvet red petals of the roses he gave me as I watch Mom and Dad through my bedroom window. They walk to the car with her leaning against him. He even opens the car door for her.

Parents hugging or kissing is just gross and I'm glad I don't see a lot of that. They live their boring grey lives with the occasional yelling match. It's what I'm used to. It's what's comfortable.

This hand holding and leaning is not.

chapter 25

I awake the next morning early, with no headache or swirling stomach — maybe going to bed at seven last night knocked it out. Then I head for the laundry room hoping for some clean underwear. I grab the dryer handle and tug the door open. No clothes inside the dryer. But then something makes me stop and look at the dryer door. Yes. It's a real handle. No wire, no duct tape, just easy opening and closing. It's such a small, stupid thing, but I almost feel a lightness.

Then it hits me again. I got caught shoplifting yesterday in front of the whole school. My picture is hanging on a Wall of Shame in that horrible store.

Even as I collect the dirty laundry and throw it in the washing machine, I keep wondering how I will get through the day, what I should wear, how I should hold myself. Can I manage not to cry?

To pass some time, I flip through the magazine that claims Jay is a Love Dove, trying to think of anything but my own life, even if it's my homework for a change. What is the market for this magazine? It's one of the "criteria" Ms Smyrnious wants us to address when we design our own magazine. I browse for the ads — they're supposed to provide the clue. But there are so many of them! Nail polish, jeans, jeans, shoes, jeans, lip colour, concealer, jeans, eye shadow, acne wash, nail polish, jeans, hair colour, jeans, hairspray, perfume. That's just in the first twenty-five pages.

Well, it's definitely for girls who like casual wear. The other stuff? Hmm. You'd think it was a magazine for girls who need a lot of help in the looks department. Ugly girls who need to get rid of baby fat — there's an article on that. Or who need help with their love lives — there's the quiz and a tear-out *Hot Date Handbook*. Girls who want to read about other girls who have even more embarrassing things happen to them — The Tell Everything Column. *I* like these magazines, though, and I'm not ugly.

My mind can't think about that too long. I start to wonder about Jay. He actually hit a guard? I can't believe it. What kind of trouble is he in? What's his father going to do to him this time? And then I feel Dad's words punch into my stomach again. *I don't ever want you to see Jay again.* How can I explain that to Jay? And just how lonely will it be without him? Maybe he is Toenail Sludge, but he's always been *my* Toenail Sludge.

I get dressed when my underwear is mostly dry, throwing on — what else? — a pair of jeans and a plain white sweater set. No colour accents at all. Just a bit of clear lipgloss and some mascara.

By that time my parents are up and on the go. Mom leaves for work early and I take the lift anyway.

I can't hang around the schoolyard with everybody staring at me so I head for Lee's Convenience, half-expecting to see Jay. But there are no kids in the store at all. I see the display of the Children's Hospital Charity Bears and remember the one Jay stole for me, smiling. I reach into my jeans pocket for my lunch money and slide it into the coin slot. There, I always meant to do that. I just never got around to it.

When I leave the store I hear someone calling my name. It's Julie. I want to turn away and keep walking, the way she did when the security guard came up from behind me. But Julie rushes after me and grabs my shoulder.

"I'm so sorry I couldn't warn you! I didn't see that woman till it was too late."

I turn to look at her and know she's telling the truth. She only did what she had to. What I probably would have done too — run away. There was no point in both of us getting in trouble. Still, that friendship quiz from *Teen Fashion* comes back to me. The Best Kind of Best Bud. How to Tell if You Are One. I remember my category: Loner. I think Julie would probably fall into that category too. I frown. We're just two loners hanging out together, not really best friends at all. And at that moment, I feel lonelier than I've ever felt in my whole life.

Julie keeps talking, avoiding my eyes now. "I'm sorry you missed your *Ms Mode* appointment too, but here, I brought you this." She hands me a pamphlet.

"What's this?" It looks like an ad for a modelling school.

"I didn't tell you, but I had an appointment with *Ms Mode* too." Julie shrugs her shoulder.

"You what? And you went? But . . . " I'm lost for words. "How *could* you?"

"It's not what you think. I wanted you to win and I never thought I would. It's just, you got to see a real photo shoot when you signed on with Ms Chev. I wanted that kind of experience too."

I start to look at the pamphlet. "They gave you this?"

She nodded. "There were three hundred girls with the same appointment in a huge hall. We listened to this big spiel about the *Ms Mode* modelling school and how it prepares you for an exciting career."

"That's all it was?"

"Then they showed us a video of the school. From there, we were all called to different rooms and pressured to sign up. It was so much money and I didn't have my parents with, so I got to leave quickly."

"Just another scam."

"You didn't miss anything. I thought you'd want to know that. I know you're grounded and everything, but at least it wasn't the big deal you expected."

I look at her and remember the way she raised her arm to wave yesterday, then the way her face turned as she rushed away. My loner friend, the Bulldozer, *now* she tells me the humiliation was all for nothing. Maybe I should feel better. Instead the world looks greyer and more boring than ever.

I head for class last minute, expecting the crowds to part away from me, whispering and snickering. Only for some reason there's nothing.

There's no Jay around anywhere either. I start to feel really uneasy. Maybe the security guard hurt him.

In class Ms Smyrnious starts talking about how hard it is to be a teen today. "You're all under a lot of pressure. I hope if something ever troubles you, that you come to me or some other adult who can help you."

Oh, no — here it comes. My stomach clenches along with my shoulders. This has to be the opener to a shoplifting discussion. Will it be about me, or Jay? Maybe he's even in court today. But everyone will still link us together. Lots of kids know by now about my brush with Economart Security.

Yada, yada, yada. Suddenly Ms Smyrnious talks

about Andrea. What? Huh? What's up with her?

"I don't know how to tell you this except to just say Andrea is very ill." Ms Smyrnious chokes up. "And we should try to remember her in our thoughts and prayers."

"What's wrong with her?" Emily asks.

Instead of answering directly, Ms Smyrnious talks about some of the harmful effects of stress: alcoholism, drugs, nervous breakdowns.

A shiver runs down my spine. Did Andrea try to commit suicide?

Then finally Ms Smyrnious introduces the words *eating disorder*.

Andrea's in the hospital from too much dieting, I think. Wow, I didn't think she had it in her. Well, now she can stop, right, so what's her problem?

" . . . doctors fear she may have done permanent damage to her heart. There is a . . . a possibility she may not make it."

No! I shiver again. I can't believe it. Andrea has always been a major geek, but she can't have dieted to death. Can't the doctors heal that? I mean, she's only fourteen. No one dies at fourteen, do they?

Ms Smyrnious passes around a huge card for us to sign. As it goes up and down the rows, she explains that Andrea won't be returning to school, but that if she pulls through she'll be moving to Vancouver with her dad.

Gee, divorced parents, that sucks. The card drifts closer and closer. Lauren finally gets up and hands it to me along with a look — like *I'm* Toenail Sludge. Okay, I was not the nicest person to Andrea. I'll be the first to admit it. I feel really bad that she's sick. But I never told her she looked good when she started losing the weight, like everyone else did. I was just as mean as when she was the size of a barge. They're all as much to blame as I am.

I look at the card and chew my lip. It's got a whole pile of strange-looking people holding brightly coloured balloons. They're squeezed into an elevator and they're looking glum. *Heard you were in the hospital,* the words across the top read. As you open the card the people step out of the elevator and release the balloons. "We've set our sights high." The glum people look up towards the balloons. The largest three have the words GET WELL SOON across them.

Boy, talk about stupid cards.

Some of the kids have drawn little things — happy faces, hearts and flowers — along with their signatures. Others have written little verses: *Yours till the butter flies, Use a smile as your umbrella — you're going to need one in Vancouver!, Happy trails, Andrea!* That one came in a lasso attached to a cowboy on a horse.

I'm no good with funny sayings. Well, I could

sketch a really cool outfit and accessories, but I know that won't work for this kind of thing.

My shoulders bunch back even more and there's a knot between my blades. *Permanent damage to her heart . . .* Geez, why did she have to do that to herself? I shut my eyes, wishing that I had been nicer to her. But it wasn't only me, honest. Nobody really likes Andrea. Even Ms Smarty Overalls Lauren Dreyburgh avoided her if she could help it, and Lauren was really her only friend. Andrea is a loner too. I open my eyes again and write my name and then one word after: Sorry. I pass the card along.

Ms Smyrnious lets us work on our own for math class. Seems like she's just not up to teaching us today. Instead, I start to scribble down some ideas for a quiz in the magazine I'm designing. *Model Girl,* I'm calling it. Are you a happy camper? How well do you deal with stress? What's your depression quotient? Yeah, that's a good one. Now some questions for it:

You wake up in the morning and:

(a) jump up to jog around the block.

(b) cover your head and hope to sleep forever.

(c) worry about how you will get through the rest of the day.

You look in the mirror and:

(a) see only the flaws you want to fix, with as much make-up as possible.

(b) smile. Just like your reflection, the rest of the world will smile back.

(c) shut your eyes. You hate the person who's staring back at you.

In your daydreams you often:

(a) regret what you've done and said and mentally kick yourself over it.

(b) replay scenes from your life, giving yourself a bigger and better part.

(c) look forward to a future achievement or goal, feeling optimistic and happy already.

The most exciting thing that you look forward to is:

(a) nothing. Your life's a mess.

(b) school ending — but hey, it's only September.

(c) sunrise. Every day is an adventure.

It sounds like I'm turning into a really terrific writer, but it's easy when I have stacks of magazines to copy. There's a certain style and some key phrases. Plus, it's easier to write a depression quiz when my own quotient is so high right now. I think I fit into the highest category. Hmm, what should that be called? Sad Sister, Melancholy Miss, Down in the Dumps Dame? — the magazine quizzes like to use alliteration, as old Smyrnious puts it. Anyway I know how it should read, bright and bubbly to cheer up the depressed person:

Things are sometimes darkest before the dawn. Why don't you make a list of the positive things

> in your life and hopefully this will cheer you up. But if you still feel depressed tomorrow, perhaps it's time to seek counselling from a friendly adult or even a professional.

I take a deep breath and let it out. If only Jay were around, I wouldn't need any counselling. Jay would take my dull grey world and colour it. Jay would cheer me up. Only, even if he were here, I wouldn't be allowed to talk to him.

I bury my head in my arms.

chapter 26

In family studies I trim all the lose threads from my dress and then my extra project is all done. I want to think about the other categories for the answers in my quiz, but Ms Ferris tells me to go and help Stephanie.

She's trying to stuff this disturbing looking pillow pet. It's either a bloody tadpole or a cooked lobster.

"Um, you were supposed to turn it right side out first," I explain to her. "What is it exactly?"

She rips all the stuffing out with a vicious yank. "My own design. Road kill," she tells me. "Like it?"

I have to smile. As she flips it back the right way and restuffs it, I think about how to create the right mouth for her flattened creature. I grab some bits of white felt Ms Ferris has in her project kit and clip them into teeth. I look over to see Steph having trouble hand-stitching the last bit of opening. "Your thread is way too long, Steph. Here." I trim her thread and whip-stitch the hole for her.

By the time we're finished, her dead red thing has a grimace of agony for its mouth, googly button eyes and a couple of black dots for nostrils.

"Wow, you're really good at this creative stuff," Stephanie says. "Check it out, Lauren."

I step back a little, waiting for Ms Smarty Overalls to say something snappy, maybe something about how mean I was to Andrea. But she doesn't. Instead she reaches out and touches the pillow pet. "Neat." Then she turns and holds something up for me to see, some kind of green lump. "Hey, could you help with my frog?"

I raise my eyebrows. "I don't know, Lauren. He looks pretty far gone."

She laughs and her gums show as usual. But I don't mind as much. *She's laughing at something I said, and she's asking for my help.* I smile too. "First off we're going to have to add more stuffing . . . "

While I'm working with Steph and Lauren I don't feel like such a loner. I even forget to miss Jay. But then later as I head for the cafeteria and he's not slamming down his books on the table, stuffing himself or ogling any girls, the tightness hits my chest and I find it hard to swallow. What's happening to him? Why isn't he back at school yet?

"Earth to Kim." Julie waves something in front of me at the table. "Have a look at this." She places the photograph she's waving in front of me. "It's that picture of you I took the day of the Detel audition," she says. "I just finished the roll yesterday."

I look and I'm shocked. It's not really me. It's Barbie in the flesh, sparkly blond hair pushed back with a pink band, white button earrings, eyes bluer than the sky. She's wearing a soft pink sweater and a crisp matching mini along with white shoes picking up the tiniest bit of pink with the butterflies in the front. "Those Detel people are nuts! They should have picked me."

Julie nods and taps the photo with a finger. "You do look fantastic. Ten times better than that Barbie in the mall."

I shrug my shoulders and start to push it towards her.

She slides the photo back. "Keep it. Do you want the negative? Maybe you should blow it up for your frame, instead of that glamour shot."

I shrug my shoulders again, then nod. "Thanks, that is a good idea."

"You heard from Jay?" she asks as I tuck the snapshot and negative away.

"No. I'm not allowed to see him anymore."

She smiles just a little in sympathy, then pushes her fries at me. "Have some?"

"No thanks," I slide them back.

She chews at one herself. "Wait a while." She waves the rest of the fry at me. "It's almost summer. Then how exactly can your parents keep you apart?"

I sigh and shake my head. I don't have the heart to think about sneaking around again. Even to see Jay.

When I get home that afternoon, Mom is waiting. She has a large photo album on the kitchen table and she asks me to sit down. "Have a look," she says and flips it open.

I stare at the person in front of me. She looks like a Seventies version of me, only different somehow. Here's a pose of her in a red backless gown, leaning back as though laughing while kicking a long leg forward. On the next page there's another picture of her in a white bell-bottom pantsuit, perched on the edge of a stool. A bathing suit shot shows her lying on something that looks almost like Gunther's flea-bitten rug. "Is this *you*?" I finally ask as I flip to another page.

"Yes. I was nineteen."

"But this is a portfolio, isn't it?"

Mom nods.

"Why didn't you ever show me? How come you never told me?"

Mom shrugs her shoulders. "Your father and I worried that my 'career' might spur you on."

The modelling business never changes . . . My father's words come back to me. It's what he said when he heard the Chevron Agency had closed without paying me. "When did you stop? When you had me?"

"Oh, long before you were born. I can tell you the exact date. It was November 9, 1979. Have you every heard of a mystery writer named Bryan Ellis?"

I shake my head.

"Well, he was looking for a cover girl for his next novel, *The Lingerie Murders*, and he called several agencies. They all sent models over who were to audition for him and his friends — in lingerie, of course. Then he took Polaroids of us. It felt pretty sleazy.

"Next day I looked up the publisher and called Bryan's editor, and it turned out he had very little say in the cover art. In fact, they were probably going with a *painting*, not a photo at all. I complained to the agency and they managed to get a minimum hourly rate out of him. But still we had walked around in these slinky clothes, just to amuse his friends. The fact that it ended up to be for money didn't make it any better." She looks right at me. "It was the lowest moment of my career."

I shut the album. "You were so beautiful . . . " I look at my mother now, and see someone different than the office workie who trudges off to work in store co-ordinated ensembles. "I mean, you still are."

"Thank you. But that's not what this is about." She takes my hands and holds them. "What I wanted to explain to you is how awful modelling can be sometimes. And I was twenty when I encountered Bryan Ellis — old enough to deal with it. You're only fourteen." She strokes my chin. "I gave you the glamour birthday shots just for fun, and always hoped that would be enough for you. You are beautiful and you don't have to prove it by modelling. Constantly competing with your looks only makes you feel less and less pretty."

Now she hugs me. "Oh, Kim, these are all things I should have said when you first told me you wanted two hundred dollars for professional photos."

I wouldn't have listened. I open my mouth to admit that, but right then the doorbell rings.

Mom watches me for an extra moment, waiting. But then the bell rings again and she sighs. "Would you get that?"

I nod and head down the hall.

When I open the door I can't believe my eyes. It's like Ken is standing on my porch. Really tall, with dark short hair just a little tousled — mousse? — he has a cleft chin, a wide jaw and even dimples when he smiles. He's smiling right now. "Hi, I'm Kyle Watts . . . "

My mouth hangs open for a second.

"Your math tutor," he continues.

"Right . . . Right! I forgot that you were coming today."

"I can come another time if it's not convenient." He blushes a great pink tone that sets off his blue eyes perfectly.

"Oh, no." I step to the side and wave him in. "Please come inside." I show him to the dining room table. "Let me get my backpack."

222

I rush back with my things and I'm just a little breathless as I unload my books on the table. My magazine folder slips out and Kyle raises an eyebrow.

"You've got Smyrnious, don't you? Guess she still gives that project every year." Kyle touches the folder. "Mind if I have a look?"

"Go ahead. You had Ms Smyrnious?"

"Uh huh. Hey, these ads you've designed are great." He picks up my Barbie photo. "Where's the Before shot?"

"Oh, nowhere. It's not . . . " Then I think to myself, What a great idea! I'll get one of those awful artsy black-and-white snapshots of me and use it as a Before. Then the Barbie one can be the After.

"Well, it's no wonder you don't understand math. Ms Smyrnious used to bore me to death."

I find myself really liking Kyle and I relax.

"We'll start with something you have the least trouble with and we'll build from there." Kyle talks to me as though I'm not stupid. We tackle problem solving, and he helps me get the answers, using the right steps so that I don't have to prove it backwards. We do about ten problems and he starts packing up.

"That's it?" I ask him. My brain doesn't feel all tangled up in knots, the way it usually does in Smyrnious's math class. I actually feel bubbly, excited. I almost want to do more.

"For today, you've done great. I'm coming over every day just for a short while. I mean, that's okay with you, right? It's what your dad agreed to." Again that lovely shade of pink touches his cheeks. He's an easy blusher.

"Yeah, sure, that's fine with me."

He leaves then and Mom nabs me as I drift back through the kitchen. "That seemed to go well."

"Kyle's great. I wish Dad would have thought of him sooner."

Mom smiles. "You might have earned an A in math."

I shrug my shoulders. "You never know."

"While you were working, your teacher called."

I shut my eyes. *Just when things are starting to look up.*

"Your family studies teacher, Ms Ferris. She wondered if you'd consider assisting her with a junior sewing course at the community centre."

"Well, I like Ms Ferris . . . "

"But you still have your heart set on modelling?"

I shrug.

"Listen, Kim, you know how badly it turned out for me. But if you still want to try modelling, despite all I've told you, I'll take you to a *reputable* agency this summer. It won't be easy. You'll have to go to lots of open calls, and I'd really prefer you to wait till you're sixteen."

Now that Mom isn't totally against me, I have to ask myself: Do I want to try modelling again? I think for a moment. With my parents on my side, it might be different. But then I think about modelling the bad fabrics and styles at Valentino and Durkin's, about trying out for the Barbie job, posing for Gunther, even for Julie. I know I enjoyed the buzz that went around the school, the way everyone looked at me and treated me special when they heard. But when I think about it, I have to admit I never once enjoyed any part of the modelling *itself*. Finally, I shake my head. "I think I'd rather help Ms Ferris."

"Great!" Mom smiles and pats my hand. Then she pulls away a little. "Jay called."

"Jay?" I can feel my face lighting up, and I'm dying to run to the phone and return his call . . . but then everything inside me sinks when I remember. No phone calls.

"He called from a pay phone and I told him you were grounded. He says he'll see you at school tomorrow."

"At school? He'll be back? That's great." Everything lifts inside me.

"Kim, the boy is always looking for trouble. We don't want you near him when he finds it. You are to stay away from Jay. Do you understand me?"

I nod. I do understand exactly what my parents want.

chapter 27

At least I don't have to worry too much about everyone at school talking about me, what with Andrea's and Jay's problems. Carlos rushes up to me the minute I near the school the next morning.

"Did you hear what happened to Jay?" Carlos doesn't look like he feels sorry for Jay. He's all breathless and his eyes flash. It's as though he's on some kind of roller coaster rush.

"He stole a CD and punched out a security guard?" I say, hoping to steal some of his glory.

"Yeah, but that's not all. His dad wouldn't pick him up when he called. Jay had to spend the night in jail."

"Oh no, poor Jay!"

Carlos looks around first and then continues in a rush. "Then there was a big scene when his father finally showed up at the station. The cops had to get between them."

I wince.

"And then Jay took off," Carlos drops to a whisper now. "He's hiding out at my house. He says for you to meet him at the gate at quarter to eleven."

I frown. Family studies class. I like Ms Ferris. I

don't want to lie to her to cut class. But what can I do? I have to see Jay, no matter what my parents say. Whether he's a perfect Love Dove or Toenail Sludge, he's my friend. I can't just desert him.

So I work at my magazine project in language arts, passing time. I figure out more categories for my Depression Quotient Quiz. I decide on Moody Ms for the middle score group and Chirpy Chick for the happiest quiz takers. Today I'm a Moody Ms:

> Sometimes you feel so bored you want to fast forward through your life. Press the FF button and finish school. FF again and you have your own place, your own car, your own life. You have a career, maybe even get married. Only then you're afraid you'll become just like your parents. On your good days you realize, maybe that's not so bad ...

I stop and chew at my pen for a moment. I see my parents holding hands and leaning on each other.

Then I write the embarrassing moments column. I write a few stupid ones about burps and stuff, some about stains, the favourite magazine ones — diarrhea and blood. But I know the four-star ultimate hide-under-a-rock humiliation is something I don't want to share, being caught shoplifting and dragged through the store in front of kids from school. I chew my pen again.

The bell rings and I know I have to duck out now if I want to see Jay. As I head to the exit I bump into Ms Ferris.

"Hello, Kim. Shouldn't you be going the other way?" She smiles at me and I don't want to lie.

I look her in the eye. "Yes. I should. But there's something I have to take care of. Some*one*, actually." Before she can answer I run for the door, push through it and keep running.

Jay's standing at the gate just the way he said. Only he looks scruffy, wrinkled and grey. There's a purple swelling around his left eye.

"Kim," he calls to me, his arms stretched out.

I grab onto him and hug him tight. Then I finger his eye. "Did that security guard do this to you?" No wonder he punched her in the nose then.

"Nah, this is my dad's work."

I wince and kiss it gently.

"Everyone loves him, but he's not what they think. He's just one big lie. He's doesn't care about my mother or me. Or my sister or brother. He acts like he's the big kiddies' pal, but then he does this." Jay points to his eye.

Jay sounds angry, but I can hear that he's close to crying too. "Forget your father," I tell him and kiss him on the lips. He kisses me back, only it's hard and desperate.

I pull away to breathe. "But what about you, Jay?"

"Well, there's no way I'm going back home. Forget that. He thinks he can make me do whatever he wants, he's got another think coming. *He's* the one who needs to learn a lesson . . . " Jay takes a quick wipe at the tears sliding down his cheeks.

"Forget him, Jay. What are *you* going to do?" I ask him again.

"I'm taking off. It's summer anyway. I'll find work."

"But you can't just lose your whole year — "

He kisses me again. "Come with me, Kim," he whispers.

Does he mean just to cut class today, or to take off for the summer? I pull away a little. I see his rumpled hair and his wrinkled clothes, the bruise on his face and the hurt in his eyes. I want to make it all better for him, I do. Because he's made things better for me lots of times.

But I don't feel any pink bubbles rising inside me anymore.

I remember the lowest point in my life, being dragged through that Economart, and I know that his way's not exciting. It's just low. And I can't see leaning on him the way my mother leaned on Dad the other day. It would never feel totally safe to be with him.

"Don't go, Jay, please. Come to my house after school. My mother won't mind if I tell her what's happened. My dad can straighten things with your father. I know he can." *My parents may be boring, but they're always there for me.*

"Come with me. Please." Jay looks into my eyes,

and I want so badly to give him the answer he's looking for. To make it okay for him.

I step forward, feeling helpless. What can I do? I don't even want to cut family studies. Then I hear Ms Ferris call. "Kim, Jay, come in now. It's time for class."

Jay starts to run.

"Come back, Jay. It will be all right!" I call after him. But I watch as he just keeps running.

I step towards the school now, but halfway to the door I stop and turn to look back one last time. Jay's at the end of the block now. Then he turns the corner and I can't even see him anymore.

Am I doing the right thing? Who can ever tell? It's not like this is a choice in a magazine quiz, where you know by the wording which is the right answer. And even if you choose wrong, you just end up in some strange category. Does anyone really fall into the perfect category anyway? Maybe Lauren's right, magazines *are* full of perfect lies.

I turn around again and walk towards the door.

Sylvia McNicoll is the award-winning author of *Bringing Up Beauty, Walking a Thin Line, Jump Start, Facing the Enemy, More Than Money, The Tiger Catcher's Kid, Blueberries and Whipped Cream, The Big Race* and *Project Disaster*. She also writes a series of books under the pen name of Geena Dare.

Sylvia is always in demand for visits to classrooms, and has worked as an on-line writer in residence. You can check out her website for more information on her books:

http://netaccess.on.ca/~mcnicoll